LIBERTY CALL!

©

Written By: Waleed Naeem Yaser   November 14, 2011

This story is not prophetic but, simply a story that injects upon society some of the many morally deviant character issues that face it. It's the greed, mistrust and deceptive fashion upon which people eat off of each other just to get the ups on the weak. It also points the prevaricator finger at the elitist in this Nation, whom have done nothing but enriched themselves at the expense of the poor and middle class. This night on the town starts with three men; two of which can only be dethroned by Congress itself - Master Chief and Senior Chief Petty Officers – along with a Chief Petty Officer.

'It started out for us, like many of the other weekend calls of liberty; but, this past weekend turned out to be anything but normal.'

"LIBERTY CALL, NOW LIBERTY CALL – LIBERTY CALL FOR ALL EXCEPT DUTY GROUP FOUR – NOW, LIBERTY CALL!"

The Duty Officer's voice over the intercom echoed about the ship. All scurried about the ship dressing up for the weekend stay in New York City.

Master Chief (MC) Forster, Senior Chief (SC) Diaz and I Chief(C) Petty Officer Naeem, were a 'Pack' true to partying till we dropped dead!

It was Friday Night, and the dinner in the Chief's Mess was being cleaned up by one of the mess deck personal. The three of us sat there smoking on Cuban Cigars, contemplating what our weekend would look like. After about an hour of debating – Master Chief won out and set our agenda for that evening.

MC: "We meet on the Fantail at 2100 hour from there; we'll drive the rental car to Little Italy and hit some of the bars there. Afterwards, we'll walk into Chinatown and see what we can get into."

SC: "They have many college girls that hang out down in Little Italy on the weekends – don't forget your 'Viagra' pills Master Chief – better to have the edge with honeys who are oversexed like them college girls."

C: "I'm driving tonight so, I won't be drinking! Just don't bother me if my Hashish clouds up the inside of the car. I've been holding on to this Turkish stash for well over two months now."

The three of us 'Shit, Showered and Shaved' before meeting out on the Fantail, as the Officer- Of- The-Day saluted both Master and Senior Chief as they walked down the Gangplank; where I had already been waiting in the rent- a- car.

We drove across the Verrazano Bridge from the Ammo Depot Base in Earle, New Jersey and headed up the BQE (Brooklyn-Queens Expressway) into Manhattan. It was almost 10 p.m. when we found parking on Mott Street in Little Italy.

C: "You two go ahead inside while I park the car. Try and get a table away from the front door, so we can look over all the prospects coming in!"

Master and Senior Chief both got out of the car and walked into the bar. I had driven half a block, when I noticed this Chinese man pointing to a parking spot. I parked and handed the old man a five dollar bill, and headed towards the bar.

When I got inside, I looked about for Master and Senior Chief – there towards the very back they both sat – they both had already started drinking when I sat down.

C: "You guys hooked into any prospects for our enjoyment tonight yet?"

SC: "Naw, little brother; it seems like all the crumbs are leftover – let's just get our drink on and head down the street."

MC: "Yeah; they all look underage to me – better we walk into Chinatown – they always have women with experience ready to do anything your pockets can pay for. Maybe after Chinatown we can head up to

Harlem and cop some Coke."

We sat there for more than an hour just watching the

prudish young Anglo girls come and go. Leaving, we

walked past the car and headed across Canal Street

into Chinatown. I had then noticed that same old

Chinese Man.

He motioned to me again as I walked over to where

he stood.

C: "Hey Pops; what's on your mind tonight anything

else I can do for you?"

'Old Chinese': "Here sonny; take this address and go

have all the fun for a lifetime – but, remember to

keep to the time scheduled or you might miss what's

coming to you."

I took the paper from his hands as he walked across

the street. I glanced at the paper and saw five

address and times posted to each one – looking back

across the street at where the old man should've

been, he had disappeared just that quickly. I got the attention of Master and Senior Chief and gave them the paper to look over.

MC: "What's this paper about Chief – what are these address and times listed here for?"

C: "This old Chinese man gave it to me, and said I should keep to the scheduled if I want the ultimate pleasures. Let's just try out and see if he's speaking the truth or just jerking my chain!"

SC: "What's the first address on the paper? And, what time are we to be there for all this fun times?"

C: "The address is 150 Pike Street – which is a few blocks from here –and, we have less than four minutes to get there. Let's walk and no lagging behind."

The three of us double stepped it until we were standing outside of the front door. Knocking we waited to see who'd respond before the time would pass.

After standing there for several minutes, the door opened and this Chinese woman answered. She invited us to enter and so we did.

Chinese Woman: "Come in and remember to keep to the schedule – enjoy yourselves here as, there's no restriction on whatever you ask or need from our women. Now, get busy as your time is short!"

Entering into the dark, candle- lit rooms – Master Chief sat down with three beautiful Chinese girls, as they poured drinks from an unmarked bottle. Senior Chief walked into a room where the Opium candle was burning and laid down with two naked ladies. I found a place near the window and sat at one of the tables and lit my pipe. I was smoking Hashish for about two minutes, when this one beautiful full figured Chinese woman came and sat in the chair next to me.

'Lady Liu': "What brings the three of you men here tonight? We don't normally get the likes of you here, mostly old Triad Gangster visit this establishment."

C: "Well, I was just crossing the street when this old Chinese man handed me this paper, and told me to follow what was written on it and not to be late in arriving at each location. Anyway, I'm just here to enjoy the pretty ladies like you! Want to try some Turkish Hashish?"

'Lady Liu': "Sure, why not! If there's anything else you want from me don't hesitate to ask me. Tell me, is it really true what they say about Black Men?"

For the next two hours the three of us played with these women in all fashions believable. Senior Chief was being served Opium by the two women, who oiled down his body and rode it like a Surf Board.

Master Chief was under the table giving pleasure to one woman at a time, as he sipped on one of the many drinks on the table.

C: "Get on top of my lap, Lady Liu – feel yourself what Black Men pack in our pocket – now, puff on the pipe baby!"

It was just before reaching my climax, that the lady of this establishment came and informed us of the time. We had less than thirty minutes to get to the next destination, which meant our fun was now over. We all dressed and gathered ourselves and walked out of the front door. Down on the street curb we hailed a passing cab and got in.

MC: "What's the next destination we're supposed to be at and, at what time should we be there?"

C: "It says: 399 Hudson Street – which is not far from here – with no traffic in front of us we should be there in less than ten minutes. It is now eleven p.m.

and the schedule says by 11:15 p.m. no later. Driver, take us to 399 Hudson Street and get us there quick." There was not much traffic, so we made it in time enough to stand outside the building and monitor the coming and going of people into the building. It looked like all the patrons were upper class Anglo Women with money. This surely was the right spot for us instead of the bars in Little Italy. We stood at the door waiting for the time to come, when Master Chief called out the hour at hand.

MC: "It is now 11:15 p.m.; ring the bell Senior Chief!" A few seconds later the door opened and there stood a middle age man, who invited us to come in.

'Man': "Come in Gentlemen and make yourselves at home! Just remember to keep your own time here – we have many like yourself who are here under the same restraints – it is all about the good times and free sexual expressions that we cater to. All is paid

for by the paper which you hold within your hand –
enjoy your evening!"

It dawned on me when he walked away – how much
like that old Chinese man he resembled – but, then
again maybe not. Like the other establishment we
just left before this one; we all split up and made our
presence felt upon the many beautiful women.
Finding a seat empty in the back, I sat and waited to
see which one of these women really felt
adventurous to swing with an Afro- American.
I was just lighting up my pipe filled with Hashish,
when a Blonde with long hair and long legs, sat down
with me. One could see she wasn't an American,
most likely a Scandinavian with big blue eyes. When
the scent from her body reached my nose bypassing
the smoke- I wanted her to stay all night with me. It
was then that I noticed on the table in the middle of
the room a pile of Coke maybe three inches high,
which people around the room took ashtrays from

their tables and filled it. I looked at her and decided I would do that same. Taking an ashtray, I walked to the table and scooped up enough to last an hour at the most.

The two of us filled our noses with this wonderful powder and sipped on Wine, as we engaged in foreplay leading to a trip to the many mini rooms in the back. Each had a ample size bed and wine cooler. I had lost all sense of time while in the arms of this woman, that, I had to be dragged out by Senior Chief, who had been keeping the time, so as not to miss out on the next adventure happening that night.

SC: "Come on little brother, finish up and get dressed. We've got less than an hour before rendezvousing at our next doorstep."

I took another ten minutes with my lady of the night and started to get dressed. She laid there and watched while playing with her nipples.

Blondie: "You're on your way to the next destination, uh! You could stay here with me and gain what mysterious wealth you're out here looking for. My father is a Billionaire and can care for us forever so, there's no need for you to continue! I will have your baby after this night – it has been written for us only if you stay with me now! Which will it be – you must choose now!"

I looked at her with astonishment for her words concerning the birth of a baby and we've only just met. I knew she was either crazy or she had some intuition concerning my future. But, I wasn't here for that; I just wanted to have fun!

C: "Listen honey, we had our fun but it's over for now okay! If by chance we should ever meet again, let's continue this matter we were forced to discontinue."

I continued to dress all the while looking down at her and the beauty she possessed. Was this a mistake to leave her or to allow Master and Senior Chief go it on their own. I decided to travel this path tonight with my two friends; instead of accepting this invitation of this lady.

MC: "What took you so long to come out Chief? We can't let these distractions of pleasure keep us from completing this list to the very end. One does not know what is truly involved in the final outcome of this evening. Now, let's get into a cab and head to our next destination."

I hailed a cab and gave him the next address written on this list.

C: "Cabbie; take us to 110 Bleecker Street. We have twenty minutes before we have to get there, so, no hurry!"

SC: "Forster, what else can we expect other than what we've already experience so far. The drugs and sex for one night can only go so far, before one grows weary of it! I hope this next stop has something very special to offer us."

MC': "I have no problem with the sex and drugs brother Diaz, as long as it's free! I haven't spent a dime so far, and if this continues for the remaining destinations, then, I'll just go with the flow! I got my bottle of Viagra here, so no problem with getting it up!"

SC: "Well, I just hope this next stop is a little different than the past two! Sex is okay; but there's got to be more than this for us to do! What are your thoughts little brother?"

C: "You know, that lady I was with had promised me to live off the money of her father and to stay and care for this child we would have after this encounter of tonight. How could she know she was pregnant – nothing really makes sense to me tonight – as for what I think, it really doesn't matter what happens to us as long as we're safe!"

Cabbie: "110 Bleecker Street — your fare is fifteen dollars — how do you want to pay; credit card or cash?"

C: "Cash and carry, my man! Here's a five spot for your tip!"

As we stood on the curb; I turned as the cab drove away, to notice that, the cabbie was a dark- skinned Chinese with dreads who, resembled that old man from Chinatown who'd given me this list. Turning back facing the building before us; I could only wonder what awaited us from behind those doors.

SC: "Okay are we all ready? I'll ring the bell!" Senior Chief rang the bell and stepped back. The door opened and we were invited to enter by two young men wearing white shower robes. They handed us towels and robes and asked us to disrobe behind the curtains. Doing so, we three stood holding the towels.

When the two young men spoke,- they spoke in unison. "You have a choice of either male or female. You may even choose from what region of the world you'd like them to come from, and what age group. Our youngest group begins at eighteen years and goes to forty years! Okay; you first sir! Which one do you choose; male or female!"

MC: "Female and her age should be mid- 20's and, give me a Russian! I want my own chance to tear down that wall!"

'In Unison': "And what would you like sir?"

SC: "Also female; about thirty years old and Hawaiian! I love the sweet juices of Pineapple!"

'In Unison': "Lastly, sir, what is your desire!"

C: "Female, twenty years, dark skin, Brazilian, very pretty and soft to the touch!"

'In Unison': "Now that we have your preference – we offer you three types of bathing environment. One level there is mild heat and steam; second level is medium and, lastly, extreme heat and steam. There you will bathe alone with your partner – no drugs or alcohol is allowed – only massage, sex and what your mind desires. After bathing you can either join others for a fine dinner or you can just sit in the smoking room and enjoy our finest cigars from around the world. Now, enter and enjoy the evening!"

We all entered into different doorways. As I walked down the hallway, lit with scented candles, I could feel the heat rise as I got closer to my room. Entering, I removed my robe; lay down on the table which was wet with the steam that rose from the pores in the floor. I just rested my head when the curtain opened and in stepped the most beautiful woman I have ever seen – she even surpassed the blonde I had just left a few minutes ago. Her voice was meek and soft as she directed me to choose the level of heat and steam.

I chose the medium level – I wanted to see the drops of water as they appeared all over her body. Her skin was neither too dark nor too light which insinuated her beauty.

C: "My name is Khalid; and what is yours if you don't mind?"

'Young Girl': "You can call me Miriam!"

C: "Miriam I want you to lay here as I massage your body first. I want to do to you what your mind hopes leads to ecstasy felt over your total body and orgasms multiple. Here, lay on your back first –where are the oils kept Miriam?"

'Miriam': "Underneath the foot of the table; you'll find them there."

I reached under and pulled out a full bottle and began pouring oil into my hands. I started at her feet and took my time massaging each one up to the knees. I then moved upwards over both thighs –she was shaven smooth as I made my way to her waist, sticking my tongue into her bellybutton where the sweet sweat had gathered. I then mounted the table straddling her body as I continued massaging her till I reached her brown tipped nipples, which were now hard and long. The oil over her body made it easy for me to glide over her like on ice – I then rolled her over on top of me as she moved her lower body towards the excitement growing below.

HISSSS! The steam gushed upwards into the air, causing the drips of sweat to cover her body as she moved slowly on top of me. I noticed a pool of water growing beneath us, as sweat dripped from her down onto me. My body too was overcome from the heat in the room, that, I had to wipe my eyes just to maintain a clear view of her. I reached up and pulled her down to me to kiss her deeply –as we both moved in opposite directions – was an orgasm possible between us with all this heat – or was it prolonged for the pleasure we were both having. A sense of completion I could force from my head, but what about Miriam; could she hold back from releasing herself all over this table.

'Miriam': "Stand up Khalid and take me over to the wall, and place my back up against it!"

I took hold tightly to her – though almost losing my grip from the oil covering her body – we moved to the corner of the room. I held her legs and placed her back against the wall.

HISSSS! Another burst of steam filled the room as fatigue began to come over me stripping me of my strength to hold her up. I then moved to the corner of the floor where it seemed a bit less intense heat and continued to make love to her.

I was awoken by a touch to my forehead – somehow, I had passed out and was lying on the floor – the touch of her hand awoken me as her smile looked down upon me. She was covered in her white robe and the room had gone down in heat and was a little cold on my ass!

C: "Hand me my robe Miriam. Listen, did I pass out for a long time?"

'Miriam': "No, only for ten minutes. You needed the rest from all your work with me. We can continue if you want. But, if you want, you can join your friends who are waiting at the front door. I leave the decision of whether to stay with me or leave to you. We have enough room in this building to accommodate one more. My place is spacious and all substance for existence is provided forever."

C: "My friends are waiting for me and I must join them in the completion of this evening. I will come back for you after tonight and take you away from here."

'Miriam': "No, once you leave this building the offer leaves with you. I can never be seen by you again -

the next guest who wishes to stay will have me for himself. Your clothes are at the end of the hallway. I must go onto the next appointment – goodbye, Khalid, forever!"

Leaving the room, Miriam away into the darkness and disappeared from sight. I retrieved my clothes and dressed in a hurry. Walking into the parlor, I nodded to Senior Chief my readiness to leave.

As we walked down the street to the corner, where we would hail a cab I asked them about their experience inside the building.

MC: "Enjoyable to say the least – just a simple sexual encounter – nothing special!"

SC: "Yeah, I concur Master Chief Findings. Nice but nothing special – this was worse than the last two places we've been. How was yours Chief?"

C: "Extraordinary, for sure! Like nothing I've experience before from a woman. She even invited me to stay with her and live a life of joy and happiness. Which was similar to the invitation given to me to by the blonde, before this? Why I'm given such invitations and you two are not? Something is funny about this night and I wish I could get a grip to what is transpiring before me."

MC: "Yeah, no one has even offered me anything like that, they've only asked if I need more of what was before me and, I've told them to bring it on. I'm not looking for redemption in my life – just more decadence with drugs, sex and the pursuit of happiness and the American way."

SC: "I concur with all that Master Chief just said! Happiness is having too much of everything – one woman is never enough. Don't want to be bogged down with the simple way of life, you know what I mean!"

C: "Yeah, I understand you well but having someone to love and bringing forth life with that love makes living worthwhile if you ask me!"

MC: "Enough of this talking about how sweet life can be! Where's the next destination, and how much time we'll need to get there?"

C: "Huh! The next stop is at 1213 Riverside Drive and we have about twenty-five minutes before we have to be there. Someone grab a cab!"

I thought about this last offer from Miriam as we drove up the Westside Highway towards the Riverside Drive destination. All I could see in my mind's eyes was her body – what have I passed up this time – I would not reject the next offer if it presented itself to me tonight, for whatever reason. I could not allow happiness to escape me – I had only two years before my last enlistment is coming which would put me well over the twenty years needed for full retirement. I was not going to be like these two

'Lifers' – spending every waking day of my life living a life of pure nothing but taking orders and giving orders. Life was more valuable than just that.

Cabbie: "1213 Riverside Drive, Gentlemen that'll be fifteen dollars – sorry, but I don't accept credit cards only cash!"

SC: "We pay only cash my man! This street is quite dark, wouldn't you say! Are you sure this is the address; because I can't see any numbers."

Cabbie: "Yeah, this is the house. You three are the second fair I've delivered to this address this evening – now you're holding me up from making my living – pay me now if you don't mind!"

SC: "Here all I have is a fifty – give me back thirty dollars, okay!"

Walking up the steps to which looked like a Mansion built between a park and a smaller building – we rang the bell which sounded like a Gotham Church bell –

the door opened and on the other side was this young girl maybe fifteen years at the most.

'Teen Angel': "Come on in – your last to arrive – they're waiting downstairs in the basement. Walk down this hallway and turn left at the final door and go down the steps. I will come in a few minutes to take your order."

We walked down the hallway which the walls were covered with the most expensive type wallpaper I've ever seen. The wall lights were gold-plated for sure and the doors were solid mahogany covered in layers of varnish. This was a classy joint for sure and most likely had the best of whatever it was offering. Just how classy could the women be, or how potent were the drugs, or how old were the liquor that would be served to us. Yes, this was surely the jackpot we were happening to land upon.

We walked down the spiral staircase for what seemed two stories. But, when we got to the landing and entered into the only room below we understood why our descent took so long.

The room was lined from wall to wall with the best of everything. The furniture looked as though it came out of the Queen Victoria age. The rugs surely were Turkish and the lighting was Spanish or Moroccan not sure. The room was constructed this way as if it were some very rich New Yorkers speak easy back during the days of the Depression. What stories these walls could tell if we could only listen. We came in and sat down at the round table along with the other people. They all looked disinterested when we sat down and no one said anything to the other.

About that time the girl who opened the door came from somewhere and sat down a tray full of sandwiches and drinks.

Waleed Yaser

'Teen Angel': "May I take your request for alcoholic drinks, please. I will return promptly with them before the start of the game. All these men have been waiting for your arrival for some time."

Dealer: "Yes, though you didn't know – but, you could've skipped all the other locations and just come here and waited for the time to start."

MC: "Nah! I don't think I could've missed all those pleasures just to sit and watch three roughnecks for all these hours. No thanks!"

'Man': "No my friend, you don't get it! You get supplied with all that plus more. Afterwards, we all come down here for the final pleasure, which is Gambling for high stakes."

MC: "And what might your name be my friend?"

Stocks: "I'm referred to as the Broker! I buy and sell stocks from Inside Traders and we all make a killing from this. So, I'm here now based on an inside trade made earlier this week, and this is my payoff for that trade."

MC: "I'm Master Chief Forster of the US Navy and it takes an act of Congress to depose me from this position. Next to me is Senior Chief Diaz who also warrants an act of Congress. And, finally we have Chief Naeem, who can be busted for shaking his penis at a little girl! And who might you be sir!"

Pharmacist: I'm called Dr. Wills! I sell drugs from the street corners all over New York, New Jersey and Connecticut – some even call me 'Tri State' for short; because I reach out and touch everybody!"

Pimp Daddy: "They call me Slick – I have more whores walking these streets than any other pimp on the East Coast. All my bitches have checking accounts and transfer monies to my account daily. I make three million yearly which I wash at my Shopping Centers that I own around the State of New

York. I'm worth over fourteen million and I'm here to make a lot more off of bitches like you and your sailor buds. Let's get this shit started before I get bored."

SC: "Okay what's the holdup – we're here now let's play!"

Dealer: "Sorry, but we have to wait for the banker to come downstairs. The young girl has most likely informed him that the table is now full." I reached over and grabbed one of the drinks from the tray. It is very expensive liquor from the strong but mild taste it left on my tongue. The room had returned to its quiet state as all awaited the banker arrival. By the time the Banker arrived; all but three sandwiches and one drink remained.

Banker: "Sorry for the delay – but there was this problem that I had to take care of. Here, let me sit these two suitcases down and we'll begin playing." Sitting down at the table and placing the 'Chips' before him, he started from his left and asked how many chips each man needed. The ante was one thousand dollars just to get into the game. He ever had an electronic debit card/credit card machine.

He went into my account and withdrew five thousand just so I could play.

Master Chief withdrew over ten thousand and Senior Chief did the same.

Banker: Okay, sirs, let's play some Poker! Texas Hold'em is the game here tonight. The button is on the Big Sailor Boy!"

Master Chief got the button to open the first bid. He looked at his two cards and limped in with just a thousand.

The first hand was more of a feeler for the other players at the table. I was just in the game to fill the chair. The pot only grew to no more than eight thousand dollars. The next two games were now being played with attentiveness, as the 'pot' grew larger and larger; I folded and sat in my chair and watch the game grow in intensity.

Banker: "Okay let's see the 'flop' – I don't understand why the game is proceeding so slowly – I'm ready to bet, play the cards in your hand!"

MC: "There's no need to talk like that; we all play this game differently!"

Everyone at the table folded their hand, as the dealer shuffled the cards readying to deal the next game. I was now down to my final eight hundred bucks – I would play all in for this game, just to end my misery.

Dealer: "Okay men let's play Poker!"

The button was now on Pharmacist, who opened with a 3K bet.

Pimp Daddy: 'A King of Spades and Jack of Clubs' – "I'm in with 3K!"

Stocks : 'Ten of Diamonds and Eight of Diamonds – I can play and see what the 'Flop' looks like, and if I don't get anything that resembles a 'straight', then, I'll fold and get out. "I'm playing for 3K!"

Banker: " A pair of Tens – let's look at the flop –if I get a ten on the flop, then I'll stay around a bit.' "I'm in now, show us the flop."

MC: "I'm still in the game and, if you can show a little patience you'll see the flop. I see your 3K!" 'Pair of Jacks is good but on the light side.'

SC: 'Shit! Pair of Trips' "I'm out!"

C: 'All in with a pair of Eights – anyways I'm all in no, need to bet anything else.' "I'm all in, don't forget!"

Dealer: "Okay let's see the flop – we have the King of Hearts, the Ace of Clubs and the Ten of Hearts. Your bet Pharmacist!"

The Pharmacist looked at his cards for the first time before offering a bet.

Pharmacist: 'Two Queens – Hearts and Diamonds – and the flop don't do anything for me. I'll stay for the

'Turn' card only, and if I get the third Queen, I'll bet large. "Another 3K into the pile!"

Everyone else threw in the extra 3K just to get a look at the 'Turn' card!

Dealer: "The turn card is a 'Ten' of Hearts – your bet Pharmacist!"

Pharmacist: 'No help at all, but still I might squeak out a win with two Queens. Even if I get a 9 card on the 'River' I still have a straight; which is more than what these others can pull out for a win. From what I see on the table, I could pull one out here with a big bid – bluffing these assholes should be easy.' "I raise you another 5K"

Dealer: "It's your bet Pimp Daddy 5K to play."

Pimp Daddy: 'I have a pair of Kings and, if the 'River' card is a King, then, I'll have three of a kind, which should win me this game.' "I see your 5 k now, let's see the River Card!"

Dealer: "Your bet Stocks! It'll cost you 5K to see the 'River' card; are you in or out?"

Stocks: "I fold!"

Dealer: "It is your bet Banker! That'll be 5K to play!"

Banker: "I want that pot – I'll bet 5K!"

Dealer: "It's your bet now Sailor – 5K to play!"

MC: 'I want to play; but my heart says that river card is not the Jack I need to win.' "I Fold!"

C: "I'm all in, remember!"

Dealer: "Okay men; let's deal the 'River' card! We have the 6 of Diamonds! Your bet Pharmacist!"

Pharmacist: "I'll bet 8-K – I want this pot, so, if you can call me then do so or get out of this game –the pot is mines!"

Dealer: "Your bet Pimp Daddy – 8K to stay in!"

Pimp Daddy: "I fold!"

Dealer: "You have the bet with you now, Banker – what'd you say, you in or out?"

Banker: "I'll bet 8-K and raise you another 8K! Now, what's your next move, Pharmacist?"

Pharmacist: 'He's trying to push you out of this pot! There's nothing on that table that says he got me beat! On the 'Flop' he did nothing and now on the 'River' card he wants to bet big. No, he's not bluffing me out of this pot!' "I'll see you raise and raise you another 10K!"

Dealer: "The bet's on you Banker – 10K to stay in!"

Banker: "I'll see your 10K – show me what you got Pharmacist!" Throwing his hand down on the table, three 10s faced up was surely the winning hand. "Can you beat that Pharmacist – three 10s – read'em and weep!"

The Pharmacist threw his hand down and said nothing. The Banker scooped up the pot all the while grinning. He'd bluffed his way into a very large pot. Seeing this style of play and the hints of bluffing both men showed; Master Chief knew how to play the table.

The next few games would dwindle down the players to only four. Senior Chief and I would sit on the couch eating and drinking what was remaining from the tray. Another hour would go by – three in all – and one more player would be fighting to stay in the game.

Pharmacist: "Listen fellows I'm running short of cash – if the bank can loan me 30K I can continue to play."

Banker: "What! Your bag is on 'E' – if so, there are no loans that the bank can give – no collateral assets can be verified at this time! Then, I guest you'll be sitting out the next game right?"

Pharmacist: "I have more than enough money to buy up three homes like this and more. But, I didn't think I'd be losing so much so quickly. Let me make a call and I'll have half a million here in less than thirty minutes. So, if you front me the cash till then, I'll give the bank ten per cent interest – now, how's that for a business proposition?"

Banker: "Sorry, but there are no couriers which are allowed into the building, once the game has begun. Whatever you came here with as far as money, is what you can play with. Now, if you have a credit card you may get cash from your bank."

Pharmacist: "I don't carry credit cards – I'm strictly a cash and carry man – if I can't get a loan then I'll leave."

Pimp Daddy: "I'll front you a cool half million – but in return; I want your clientele list in the business district, along with the many lawyers in your back pocket. Now, how's that for a business proposition?"

Pharmacist: "It's a deal – you get to pick from the list any names you like – now, hand over the money! Deal me in the next game!"

With new money in hand; The Pharmacist was back at it – losing heavily as the approaching hour neared. The big winner was now Master Chief and The Banker. Both of them had between seven to nine million each as, Pimp Daddy's bag was almost emptied out. The Pharmacist was on the outs again, and Stocks had gone belly up. This time they would sit near Senior Chief and I to watch the outcome of the following games.

In the game which finally put Pimp Daddy on the outs; Master Chief had bluffed Pimp Daddy into going all out, where he beat him with four threes. Pimp Daddy had three Aces but still fell short. The table belonged to the two men – both Master Chief and The Banker! This was about to turn out to be something to watch.

Pimp Daddy: "Well, it looks like I'm sitting out from here on out. That leaves the table to the Sailor and the Old Fart!"

C: "Senior Chief! I was just looking at this list, and it says our next destination is a few blocks from here and we have less than one hour to get there – do you think we can make it. Master Chief is on a roll and I don't want to distract him."

SC: "Listen Chief I haven't seen him play this way for years now. The last time was back in Thailand in 1989. That's almost thirty years ago – and, he playing like he did back then – no, let him play and you go on to the next destination alone. I will be by his side until the final game is over. You have enough money to take a cab?"

C: "Yeah, I have enough cash in hand. But, I really don't want to leave you two here by yourselves. Who knows what these people will do if he wins all that money?"

SC: "Don't worry little brother – remember the Master Chief and I are Navy Seals – nothing here that we can't handle. Now go ahead and enjoy the rest of the night. Here, take a extra hundred in case."

I bided all a good morning and started up the stairway. At the front door I was let out by the teen angel, who didn't speak or hold eye contact with me. Standing on the curb I waited for ten minutes or more for a cab to pass by. But, none did so I walked up a few blocks to Broadway, where I hailed a cab.

C: "Hey, cabbie, good morning please take me to 223 West 125th Street. I need to be there within the next fifteen minutes."

Cabbie: "No problem, Sir! I'll have you there in less than ten minutes. There's no traffic at this hour so don't worry. So, how was your evening out on the town? Pick up any hotties for your pleasures; the city has too many places where one can get the edge off."

C: "Oh, I could tell you some stories about what went on tonight! You got a big ear to listen while you drive. Well, it all started out in Little Italy......"

Dealer: "Okay, Gentlemen, let's play – the bet is on you Banker."

Banker: "Who's an old fart? Just give me your money you street trash. For all the business you could have gone into, you choose to be a peddler of sex! It must be great to know you enslave women to make a living. But, I'm quite sure you're proud of yourself."

Pimp Daddy: "You are judging me old man! What did you do to own such a Mansion like this on Riverside Drive – what, take some old ladies pension fund from Wall Street – or maybe you and the Government invaded some small nation somewhere around this world. I care for my women; no druggies and they all have large bank accounts in an offshore bank. They make me lots of money and I return that with profits to help them once their lives are done in this business. I'm better than the Government Social Security plan. Now give me a break; and play cards."

MC: "I agree 'P' Daddy! Let's leave that shit alone and play cards. I need more of you guy's money. Senior Chief will you hand me a drink!"

SC: "You want a double on the rocks or straight up?"

MC: "On the rocks!"

Dealer: Okay, two cards for you all – now, the bet is on sailor!"

MC: 'Two 10's – I'll stay around awhile - I don't lose anything but their money anyway.' "That'll be 20K to stay in Banker."

Banker: 'Ok, we have a Queen of Spades, and a Nine of Spades. Nice set of cards but not to bet 20K on!' "I fold!"

Dealer: "Pot goes to the Sailor!"

Banker: "Okay ,let's up the stakes for the following games. Let's say 20K per blind – too steep for you Sailor?"

MC: "Say we do 25K per blind - dealer, deal the hand!"

Dealer: "Okay men let's play hard ball!"

Banker: 'Ace of hearts and King of Diamonds – nice hand; now let's see the flop!' "I bet another 25K – your bet sailor!"

MC: 'Queen of Spades and Ten of spades – possible flush straight – good betting hand. "I see your 25K and raise you another 25K." 'I need a good flop and I'll push a bit harder to get him out of this game!'

Dealer: "That's 25K to stay for the flop Banker!"

Banker: "I'm in for another 25K – deal the flop!"

Dealer: "Okay men; let's see the flop! The cards are King of Spades; Ace of Clubs and Nine of Spades – all black – your bet Banker!"

Banker: 'Nice! Go high and push the sailor overboard!' "I bet 50K – now what sailor, you wet yet!"

MC: "No sweating on my part Banker! The cards are reading in my direction – I see your 50K and raise you another 50K – you in or out!"

Banker: "I see your 50K now; let's see the Turn Card! Deal the card, dealer!"

Dealer: "The turn card is Jack of Hearts! Your bet, Banker!"

Banker: Two pairs – Kings and Aces – winning hand! No way is the River Card a spade – anyway, the sailor can't have anything worth betting. He's bluffing his way through this hand! I'll push a bit harder on the next bet!' "I bet – let's see, 100K!"

MC: 'The turn card helped nobody – I can't let this pot go that easy – I'm not betting with my own money anyway; so, to lose this hand still puts me up tonight! "I call you for that 100K and raise you another 50-K!"

Dealer: "That'll cost you another 50K to view the River Card, Banker! Now, are you in or out?"

Banker: 'This is it - either I win this hand or find myself hurting badly in the pockets. I'm in for almost 300 large here! "I see your 50-K and raise you another 50-K – you in sailor?"

MC: "I see your 50K and let's see the River Card!" 'Come on Jack of Spades'!

Dealer: "The River Card is Jack of Spades!"

Banker: 'No way he has a straight flush!' "Two pair Aces and Kings! Can you beat that, Sailor?"

MC: "Straight Flush! Nice hand - you almost pushed me out with that last bid but, I felt the Jack was sure to come. Seems like you're on the light side in your pockets – you still want to play?

Banker: "You seem very sure of yourself, Sailor! Remember I'm the Banker! I have unlimited assets at my control. Like those two suitcases over there. Let's say we bet half a million on the next hand and I use that suitcase for my portion."

MC: "What do I look like – some boot camp sailor still wet behind the ears – no, you got to show me what's inside first and then we'll play for your stakes!"

Banker: "This is my home sailor and I will back up whatever bet with my home and everything within it. It's just that this suitcase has a hidden prize that will take winning the next hand to view the contents. But, to see the contents of this suitcase, you'll have to bet half of what you've got there. Are you a betting man or has all this gaming been for naught. Let's play if you're gutsy enough."

MC: "Deal the cards, Dealer! I'm in for half a million!"

Dealer: "Okay men let's play cards! The bet is on you, Sailor!"

MC: 'Two Jacks in the hole – now, let's see what he's got' "I bet another 250K."

Dealer: "Your bet, Banker!"

Banker: 'Two Aces!' "I see your 250K and throw in the suitcase – that'll cost you another 500K to see the contents Sailor!"

MC: "Well, it's not my money I'm playing with anyways. I see your bet – now, let's see the 'flop'."

Dealer: "Okay gentlemen we have…. Ace of Hearts, Jack of Spades and Nine of Hearts. Your bet, sailor!"

MC: "I check!"

Banker: "I also check! Deal the 'Turn Card'!"

Dealer: "Okay, the 'Turn Card' is – Queen of Clubs – your bet, Sailor!"

MC: "I check again! Let's see what comes out of the River this time!"

Banker: "I check! Deal the 'River Card'!" 'I got him beat this time – three Aces can't be a loser hand – I get back some cash but, the case stays closed for now – well, let's see what happens first.'

Dealer: "The River Card is….. the Jack of Diamonds….we have two pair on the table. Your bet, Sailor!"

MC: "I bet another 250K – how about you adding that extra suitcase into the pot, Banker?"

Banker: "No, that case is my backup if I lose this hand! I'll expect an even larger bet to view the contents of that suitcase. Show me what you got Sailor! I have three Aces – can you beat that?"

MC: "Sure can; four Jacks beat three Aces any day of the week!"

SC: "Nice play Master Chief! We've got him going now – hand over the key to the suitcase. Let's see what's inside!"

Banker: "I said you could win the suitcase but I said nothing about having a key. That's the deal with winning these two suitcases. You'll have to open them the best way you can. I've tried but haven't figured out what to use. Maybe you can come up with something, Sailor!"

MC: "What the 'F' is going on here – you playing us like we're fresh off the boat – I say you keep the suitcase and give me the money instead. That'll be a cool million and some to be exact."

Banker: "No game fellows – it's just that, I've had these cases for over three years now, and the person I won them off of said if I could get them open I'd be rich ten times over. Well, I just gave you the winning hand of a lifetime! Now open it and get what's inside. I have some tools over there behind the bar."

SC: "I got this Master Chief – I'll get the damn thing open in no time – what do we have here as tools. Ok, drill, grinder and metal blades for cutting. Let's get a look inside!"

Pharmacist: "Hey, Pimp Daddy, what you think inside the case? I'd give the city to know what's inside."

Pimp Daddy: "It'll most likely cost that much to probably see the contents of that other suitcase. Let's see if the Sailor can open this one first!"

MC: "Can you open the damn thing, Senior Chief, or not? What you lose your skills as a Machinist – been sitting on your ass handing out orders instead of staying in the mix!"

SC: "I got this, Master Chief – this shit is boot camp – I'll have this open in ten minutes or less. Now, hand me another grinding blade for this tool – this is some hard metal for sure. I haven't see the likes of this since shutting down the 'Reactor' onboard that Aircraft Carrier in Japan, remember that one!"

MC: "Yeah, I remember for sure – you nearly got everyone killed when you almost cut through the reactor core – now, stop fussing and get this damn thing open. I want to see my winnings!" 'Look at that bastard sitting there just watching – I wonder if he really knows what's in the suitcases?'

SC: "I'm in like Flint! Holy Shit! Man, we hit it big time here – look at all that cash – must be close to two million packed inside here. Come on Brother Man; let's take the cash and split – maybe we can catch up with Chief Naeem before the night is finished!"

MC: "Man, who'd thought we hit the jackpot on a night that started out with whores and drugs- only to finish off sitting rich on the pedestal. Okay, Banker; we're cashing out and leaving – it was nice playing with you Gents but we've gotta go!"

Banker: "No, you can't leave before giving me a last chance of winning back my suitcase. I'll put up this other suitcase against that one there. One hand winner takes all! You in or out; which one is it?"

SC: "You can take this fool, Master Chief – you're on a roll so better use what luck you still have and take both suitcases on our way out. We both can hand in our resignations and go off to some far away beach and just chill. Just play one more hand for that other case. I'll get it open faster than the first one."

MC: "Okay, Senior Chief – I'll play one more hand – we win, we both retire! Okay, Banker; one more hand for all the marbles! Deal the cards Dealer!"

Pharmacist: 'Maybe I can get in on this take – I'll offer him half of Manhattan revenues for one year to have a piece of that pie.' "Hey, Sailor! I'll back you with ten million cash if you take the Banker! I'm good for the cash!"

Pimp Daddy: "I want in on this too! I'll back you for the same amount of ten large to see the Banker go down! Is that alright with you Banker – I can have the cash here in less than an hour if you win – what'll say?"

Banker: "I don't care who's in on this last hand. You lose you pay – I lose you all get a piece of what's in this case. Remember, what's in here is worth more than two or three times of the first suitcase. Let's play, Sailor!"

MC: "Senior Chief get written proof from those two 'Street Peddlers' that, they'll use their finances to cover me if I lose. Between the two of them, we'll be setup for more than the rest of our lives. Deal the cards Dealer!"

Dealer: "Okay, Gentlemen, this is the last hand for this evening! Winner takes all – one hand all in – let's play."

Banker: 'Two Kings!' "This is the destination that you all have been living to encounter and now I bring it to you and place it before your very eyes. Can you grab hold to it and make it your own or, will it take hold of you and turn your lives out! I'm all in with which is before you!"

MC: 'Two and Three of Hearts.' "Everything placed before me in on the table! Deal the flop!"

Dealer: "Okay; let's see what the 'flop' gives us! We have…. the Four of Hearts, the King of Hearts and Six of Hearts. Anyone working on a 'Flush' we have the beginning of one."

Pimp Daddy: 'What's the Banker got in the hole – he's not showing any signs of either good or bad. And, the Sailor seems oblivious to whatever he's got in his hand. This shit is nerve racking – damn glad I'm not playing; I'd be sweating by this time!'

Pharmacist: 'He's working on a flush – the sailor is working on a flush – he can't pull it off two times in a row can he? Na! The Banker has him beat – I should've bet with him – sailors are fagots anyway!

This is great drama fit for cable!'

MC: "Deal the 'Turn Card'…..!"

Dealer: "Here we go for the 'Turn Card', Gentlemen! The card is…. the Six of Hearts…. we still have the possibility of a flush and maybe a straight flush on the table."

SC: 'Master Chief has him! I see it written all over his face…. he has the straight flush…. he needs only the five of Hearts. He gets it and we have that last suitcase – I can't wait to open it to dig into it and fill my pockets.

MC: 'All these years of port calls from one country to another! Now, I can relax and enjoy the life I've been missing.' "Take me to the 'River', Dealer – so, I can wash my feet in all the riches – show me the 'Five' of Hearts!"

Dealer: "The 'River Card' is….. uh!"

SC: 'He's got it!"

Pimp Daddy: 'Shit really does come true if you believe!'

Pharmacist: 'I got a piece of that suitcase – 'F' everybody and pay me!'

MC: "I won everything – the case and all this money – hand it over Banker! Now you know what it is to play against the Master Chief! Senior Chief open the shit up and reap the bounty of a long night of work. Let's see just how much we've made!"

SC: "I'll pop this top very shortly! Hand me the grinder and stand back!"

Pimp Daddy: "Stand back, Banker – you know why not be useful and get the four of us some drinks! Hurry up Sailor boy and open the suitcase!"

Pharmacist: "Why are you standing way back there behind the bar Banker. Don't you want to see what's inside?"

SC: "That's it, it's opened! Help me peel back the metal…..what the F….. there's another suitcase enclosed within. It's looks much older than the Stainless Steel outer case. What the F is in this – no problem, I'll pop that open just as the first. Stand back!" The grinder blade started to glow white with the amount of heat it created from cutting into the old metal. "That's it I got it open – now, let me peel back the metal and….. holy shit!"

MC: "What is it Senior Chief? What's inside the suitcase?"

Banker: "That gentlemen is my 'Master' – He has been encased in that suitcase for the past 1000 years – I was unable to release him; I needed the greedy, low lifes like yourselves to do this for me – now, stand back while he comes forth to stand before you. I introduce to the World again: Gog the brother of Moog! Bow before your Master! Hell is your next destination where you'll feed the fire with the souls

my Master will gather up till the end of Days!"

Cabbie: "This is the address sir! That'll be twelve

dollars please!"

C: "This is 223 West 125th Street- this is a Bodega and

not a whore house – are you sure this is the

address?"

Cabbie: "Yes, I come here all the time for coffee late

at night! Ahmed runs this place! Go inside and ask

him if you don't believe me."

C: "Okay, I will but, I would've thought this would be

a whore house." 'Standing before the Afro- American

old man I was sure this address was not the one listed

on the paper. But, to my surprise it was. "Excuse me

brother man – but, is this 223 West 125th?"

Ahmed: "Yes it is but, you should've come with your

partners – what, you left them behind? Coming here

alone does you no good – it was for the three of you to be here and to move on to the next destination. Sorry, but you'll have to end your travels here. The list is null and void from here on out – here take this lottery card with you and cash it in tomorrow. It's only worth ten million where as it's true worth was well into nine figures – but, your partners are not here! Go enjoy what you have – all others are now forgotten!"

C: 'Leaving the store I again noticed a slight resemblance to the 'Old Chinese Man'…. but, that couldn't be!' Cabbie; take me back to where you picked me up – or could you just take me to 1213 Riverside Drive – I want to pick up my friends there."

Cabbie: "Sure can do that my man! I'll just add it on to the tab! That is 1213 Riverside Drive right? We'll be there in ten minutes or less."

Driving back towards the Hudson River we turned onto Riverside Drive.

Cabbie: "You did say 1213, right – well, I don't see 1213 on either side of the street – are you sure of the address?"

C: "Yeah I'm sure of it – I don't even see the Mansion anywhere on the street – okay then take me back to where you picked me up and I'll walk from there to the address."

Cabbie: "You want me to drive you back to East Houston Street at Katz's Restaurant?"

C: "You didn't pick me up there – it was just around the corner here that I got into the cab, right?"

Cabbie: "No buddy, I picked you up on Houston Street and you asked me to take you to Harlem. Are you alright buddy! You sure you want me to drop you off around the corner?"

C: 'This night had turned into a mystery for me. I had lost both Master Chief and Senior Chief somewhere – maybe the drugs and boozes had distorted my memory about what had happen tonight. I was sure to catch up with the two of them back in Chinatown!'

"Cabbie; take me to Chinatown. Mott Street and Canal will be good! Here's a fifty spot for all your troubles." 'I sat back and closed my eyes to view what might've happened to my memory of my two close friends.'

Cabbie: "Hey, asshole, I didn't ask you to clean my windshield – get your drunken ass off my cab!"

"I'm no asshole – I'm Gog!"

Liberty Call

A Prayer for a Dead Soul

Waleed Yaser

Written By: Waleed Naeem Yaser
November 30th 2011 ©

The year is 1917; Harlem New York and the 'Renaissance'
were in full swlng. From Jazz speakeasies to Houses of
Prostitution; Harlem was an area of pleasure, intellect,
retrospection and growth. From the Westside to the
Eastside of the East River, Harlem was jumping with
excitement.

When the Sun set and the night lights glowed – the streets
of Harlem flourished with all types of people looking for
the night's gratification. Here on Saint Nicholas Avenue,
was one of the city's best stocked whore-house. It was
managed by old lady Rue Gaul, who'd come to Harlem
back in the late 1890's from Louisiana. It is said, that she
was a 'Black Witch' who, delved into 'Zombies type
ritual's' who scared away many of those who sought to
take over her stall of women.

Many of the Mob types had tried unsuccessfully for many
years, to disenfranchise this establishment which she

started with ten of the girls she brought up from Louisiana. Rue Gaul had purchased the Brownstone building on Saint Nicholas Avenue in less than five years since moving into the area. Many of her cliental was some of New York's elite from Wall Street and City Hall. Her place was so popular because of the 'light skin women' she employed. But, on this one night in late August of 1917; things changed for the worst. Ms. Rue Gaul's place was under surveillance by the New York City Police Vice Squad. Sitting in an unmark car across from Rue's Brownstone, two Detectives watched as the many patrons entered the Brothel. They had been staked out for almost three, as the noted the coming and going of many of New York's businessmen.

Detective May: "How long are we to sit here – it's hot and my shirt is wet from perspiration – and, I'm starving for something to eat. Listen, I'm going to pick up something down the way, you want a cheese sandwich on white bread?"

Detective Orr: "Yeah, but hurry back – we have to call into the station at 11 p.m. – you aren't going to sit down in the diner are you?"

Detective May: "I was going to; but, I can bring back two sandwiches if that's the case. It shouldn't take me no more than fifteen minutes to return; so, no grandstanding.

We're supposed to just sit here and watch! I'll be back soon!"

Inside the Brothel standing behind the bar, Lady Gaul watched as the merriment of the evening was just beginning to soar. The piano player was playing the latest Jazz tones accompanied by the trumpeter and drummer; dancing by the men and women was ecstatic as they did The Toddle. The place was smoke filled and alcohol poured like water around the room, as women sat on lap after lap arousing the desire in their pockets. The stairway to the second and third floors were like a cattle drive – men in expensive suits with bottles of Champagne stuck under their arms and a lady in the other, up and down all night long. Money exchanging hands – some even being thrown at the bar, where Ms. Gaul stood, catching it and placing it under the bar.

Piano Player: "Damn good night Ms. Rue – look at them there tips in my glass – I'd be able to pay my rent tomorrow for sure! Ms. Rue! You think I can work here always. No need for me to go back to school – momma done lost her cleaning job down at them rich folks home, and she needs me to help. I can play till closing time if you want. So, do I have the job Ms. Rue?"

Lady Rue Gaul: "Well, you do play a mean piano boy; but, you only seventeen years old – what if the police raid my place and they catch you here in my establishment – they sure to charge me with corrupting a minor. But hell bent boy; you can play piano for as long as you like – but, you have to get paid on tips only. I've got too many other mouths to feed here. Between the cops and Mafia family – it leaves me little for paying my girls. Just keep slamming them ivories for these white folks dancing like they do, and all will be happy."

It was a time of newfound sensual gratification, that those with the funds could enjoy it, and they did it with grander. The Stock Market was neutral and we were in a new war in Europe. But, here in Harlem, the joint was jumping all night long! It was New Years Eve, every night and it all started over the following night. All was well in the old town tonight; that was, until they came knocking.

Detective Orr: "Where did you go for them sandwiches; The Bronx! I hope they put mustard on mines!"

Detective May: "Anything happen when I was gone? The phone-box didn't ring when I was gone did it? You know Captain Mercer will call and tell us when to go in and roust the place. He said there'll be someone coming from downtown to help us. He said they'd be wearing bowler hats with white feathers in them. Just keep an eye out alright. It's about 1 a.m. and I need to close my eyes for a second."

5

Waleed Yaser

Detective Orr: "Okay; if the phone rings or I see them white feathers, I'll wake you alright!"

Patron: "Whew we! Lady Gaul; these girls of yours know how to fill a man's pockets – been sliding in and out all night long – damn near wore me out; but, I can swing. Here; spread this around to your music players, I could hear that wonderful jazz all night upstairs with my girl. Enjoyed every bit of her – here; take a bit more for her. I'll be back Friday night with some of my Wall Street buddies – keep the girls hot and my Champagne cold! Good night – or, should I say. Good morning!"

It was well passed 3 a.m. when the phone box rang twice. Getting out to answer it, Detective Orr spoke a few words and hung up the phone. Getting back in the car, he woke Detective May from his sleep.

Detective Orr: "Wake up buddy; the white feathers are on their way here. Captain just told me to go and make an initial push at the front door. He also said that once the white feathers arrive, that, we're to leave the rest up to them. We can go home and be back at the precinct by mid-morning. Okay, let's get going before they come!"

Getting out of the car and walking across the street to the Brothel; they knocked on the door and was greeted by one of the girls.

Cynthia: "Mama Rue; there's some police at the door – want me to let them enter – or, do you want to wait on the steps?"

Lady Rue: "Open the door girl – what, police are always invited, as long as they can pay…. Ha ha ha! What you boys want tonight – you've been paid – so, why the present at my door?"

Detective May: "Uh no problem; it's just that we got a call about a shooting in the area, and we are wondering if you heard something?"

Lady Rue: "Hell man this is Harlem! You going to hear something going on round this town in these times we live in. No, isn't no shooting going on here but what's happening in them beds upstairs – so, if you want and can pay, you can go set off a few rounds of your own… ha ha ha! See you boy! Close the door girl!"

Detective May: "Sorry to bother you Miss – we'll be going now – have a good evening!"

As the two detectives were making their way back to the car; a Paddy Wagon pulled up to the front of the brownstone. Behind it came a Cadillac with the top down. Out jumped six men wearing Bowler Caps with white feathers in them. This was who the Captain said would take over the investigation.

Waleed Yaser

Detective May: *"They must be the boys from Vice! We can leave now while they clean thing up."*

Detective Orr: *"Yeah, let's say we stop off at a Deli for coffee and a hot plate?"*

Unbeknownst to the Detectives; these six men weren't from Vise at all, and the Paddy Wagon was painted to resemble one owned by the City of New York. The people entering that building were none other than the Henchman (HM) attached to Lucky Salami. He had been for years now trying to recruit Lady Gaul to work for him; but, she had always turned him down, saying, 'she go to hell before working for the mob'. Well, tonight was going to be either one or two decisions that would be made by her and her girls. There were four police in uniforms who accompanied the Paddy Wagon; and all ten men stood in front of the building.

HM1: *"Okay Boys! Listen up now; no mistakes, no shooting – the boss wants all the women inside – as for the other people working there, they are free to go as long as they don't give us shit in return. We go inside and show badges and round up every woman and put them into the paddy wagon – you got it – okay, let's do this."*

Walking up the stairs and pounding on the front door; these men were confronted by Ms. Gaul herself.

Lady Rue: *"What the hell you knocking on my door in that fashion – and why you here – your bosses got paid this week, I delivered it myself to the Captain.   This is the second time you boys were here tonight; so, why you bothering me when I'm trying to make a living?"*

HM1: "It's not for you to ask me these questions. I'm here to arrest all you women. Okay men, round them all up and bring them into the parlor. Check every room on all three floors. Here, you two officers go to the basement and bring up anyone there to the parlor. Now, you Lady Gaul go and sit down or you'll be knocked down and handcuffed – I'm here to do my job and I'm going to do just that. Round up the workers in the kitchen and here; you musicians come from over there and sit there on the floor – hands under your asses and don't move."

It took all but ten minutes to round up everybody in the building. Handcuffs were placed on the women's hand, and taken and put into the paddy wagon. The workers were led outside and told to scram! They all ran in different directions into the early morning. It was coming up on 4 a.m. when the door was padlocked and pasted with a poster – 'Out of Business' – as the paddy wagon pulled away from the curb, followed by the Cadillac, the ride downtown took only ten to twelve minutes at the most, before coming to a stop.

In the back of the paddy wagon, the thirteen women, handcuffed behind their backs, sat waiting to walk into the Station House to be booked. Lady Gaul would take care of this matter. They would allow one phone call to her lawyer, and, he'd be there in minutes with a bag of cash to release all the women. When the door to the paddy wagon opened, and there was very little light on the street, meant that they were taken to a different precinct or to the Tombs – but, the ride was very short to be lower Manhattan – so, if not lower Manhattan; where were they.

Lady Gaul: "Officer! Exactly where are you taking us! I don't remember there being a precinct in this area so close to the Hudson River – I can hear the boats on my left side. What's going on here you bastard! This isn't an arrest it's an abduction or a kidnapping – whose hand is involved with this?"

HM3: "Shut up you old witch or I'll smack what life is left in you out. Just move and don't say a word till you're told to talk; now, walk this way!"

The men led the women into a poorly lit building and down some stairs, across a corridor which was long and narrow, and then up five or six steps into this large cement walled room with one large circular light in the middle of the ceiling.

There waiting in three chairs behind a table were three of New York's Mob Bosses. Lucky Salami, Joseph Pasta and Vito Bolognese!

As the ladies were paraded in front of the table, Lady Gaul pushed her way forward to stand before these three gangsters. Looking them all in their eyes, not blinking, showing any fear, she speaks!

Lady Gaul: "So, this is what you three have been planning all the while for me and my girls. You couldn't buy me out so, now you want to kill us and take my property. Or, maybe even put some of Lucky women in to replace us – how you going to bring white women in to work Harlem – this part of the City is ours and, we isn't handing it over to you spaghetti eating Niggers. You'll have to take Harlem with blood – ours and yours will fill the gutters – is that what you want Lucky?"

Lucky: "It doesn't have to be this way Lady Rue! We've asked you many a time to come in with us for protection and you've refused us every time. Well, now that time is expired and no extension will be given. You either take our proposition or, well, we'll have to give you this location as your resting place. The choice is yours to make now Lady Rue. Make it quick so we can get along with life – you have two minutes from now!"

Looking back at her girls; she smiled giving them a sense of optimism that all would be well. She then turned and looked the Mafia bosses in their faces and spoke these words.

Waleed Yaser

Lady Rue: *"MIsfy secbula walayyah nottocillar colltetnur fihialli!"*

Vito: *"What the fuck was that – some spook speaking Africa words – this is America you bitch. Lucky; I say we get rid of these bitches. Gag their mouths and tie them up and let their bodies rut in this basement. It'll be like burying them alive; but, here they can watch each other die! Okay boys tie them up in them chairs – I'm going upstairs to get some fresh air!"*

Screams from the girls were muffle by the amount of Cement and the distance to the street. All were tied up with rope, the handcuffs removed, and gagged with handkerchiefs. The chairs were put in a circle so all could watch the other die a slow death.

Lucky: *"You should've taken my offer Lady Rue. You and your girls would still be amongst the living, but, now you're dead, in a while that is! Hell is waiting for you to come knocking Lady Rue... so, be nice!"*

When the mob left the room; they allowed the light to remain on. It was wired into the city lines, so no one would ever know the service was being used. It would stay on as long as that bulb stayed lit.

Lady Rue just looked at each and every one of her girls smiling with her eyes. Fore, she had done something that the Witches from Louisiana rarely done. That was to invoke the Dead Sprite Jumbi to reserve their souls and bodies, till time come for revenge against the families of these men. And, upon that day that their family members pays, their souls will be released from this grave and dispersed to the heavens or to hell!

As decade after decade passed by; Urban Renewal had for this area became necessary, and many buildings were torn down, some were replaced and others just became vacant lots. The building under which lay these women, had become a park, which in time passing, had been decaying from lack of the city's upkeep. Entering the 1960's , the 70's, 80's and late into the 1990's – the park had become overgrown, the benches rotting out and a fence being erected around it, to keep young people out. Y2K was the rallying call for change in America. Though it never really went anywhere, it was a slogan worth saying, if only to be a part of society during those times. But, yet another decade went by and those souls wane underground awaiting a Miracle or something like it.

PRESENT DAY BLUES

Lowdown: "Get your ass out there and bring my money! Bitch, this is your last warning; next you'll get my foot up to the knee. I didn't spend that money on your dress just to have you stand around. Now, bring back something by the end of the night or keep running!

Lowdown was just one of many Pimps on the corner, with a stable of whores to make his living. 10th Avenue and Thirty-First Street; a heaven for working girls earning what they could of a living, if this was living! It was a hot muggy night in July of 2010. The weather man had warnings of severe high winds and lighting; with a possibility of a passing Tornado. None of the girls wanted to work that night, but, their pimps had other plans for these girls.

Maxi: "Guest the best thing to do is to find you a John and make it last – better to be in a car then to be standing outside on the corner, when that storm come through."

Patti: "I hear you girlfriend – looks like the weathers about to change for the worst now. Look at them clouds coming in fast – starting to get dark as we speak – hey; look a Mercedes is slowing down – maybe you or I have that ride we were talking about. Hey Baby!" She waved at the car to come over and it did. All the windows were tinted but, you could still see inside. The window came half way down and the game was on. "What you looking for mister? You want a full moon or half – which is it?"

Mercedes: "How much for a full moon baby doll?"

Patti: "That'll be two hundred and that includes tossing your salad for you if you want!"

Mercedes: "Let's say one fifty and you can toss my salad!"

Patti: "Listen mister; if I have to toss your salad, then, it'll be two hundred! Open the door and we'll talk about it."

Getting into the car, she waved bye to Maxi; because this would be the last time Patti walked the earth. She had gotten into the car with a Serial Killer! He was yet to be known as many of his killings were done on Long Island, and now he was branching out into Manhattan. He would drive up the Westside towards Harlem, where, he would park the car in a vacant lot and torture and kill his victims. The storm was just overhead and the rain fell in sheets! Lighting crackled about and just as Patti was taking her last gasp – lighting hit near the car – lighting up from outside what was going on inside the car. Just a shadow of him over top with both arms pushing downward into the seat. And, then all was dark again. He started the car and drove off to dump the body where it could be found – Chinatown near the Brooklyn Bridge is where they would find her body the next day.

There back at the vacant lot; the lighting had enter through a small space in the manhole cover which needed a ground to stop – it went down one hundred feet, and through water another hundred feet and came to a stop in

15

the cavern where Ms. Gaul and her girls waited an awaking! When the lighting hit the back wall; the room lit up can crackled with a waking sound.

Detective Lopez: "This is the third body found here in the city. All three are known street walkers. One would think, the others would be more careful after the first girl was found."

Detective Mary Lake: "What more can we do, but hand out flyers asking them to use more precaution in their line of work, and to assist one another by making identification of vehicles used to transport them to their dates. Whoever is doing this doesn't have a problem gaining these women's trust. They get into his car and that's the last anyone will ever hear from them."

Detective Lopez: "Then, I guess we'll have to work even harder, to try and track down who's doing this. It's all a matter of time before he feels safe enough to go out and get another girl. With the same 'MO' as that of Long Island; we are seeing him branch out into different locals. Based on my assessment, he will strike here in Manhattan again, before heading to other locations. We might have only weeks to catch him or lose our chance of ever doing so. Let's stake out Hell Kitchen tonight and Chelsea tomorrow night. We'll catch this guy for sure!"

Parked along Ninth Avenue and Forty Ninth Street – both detectives sat watching the going on of the night.

Hookers range in class from low to upper high class walkers of the night. There was one in particular who had caught Lopez's eyes, from her stunning beauty and style of dress. She looked as though, she was going to or coming from a Broadway Show, but decided to stop off and earn some extra cash for the gala evening ahead. But, his attention was taken away from her to that of the elegant looking Cadillac slowly driving close to the curb. He nudged detective Lake who, wrote down the license plate number, as they watched to see what he would do.

Running the plate through the computer, turned up that of Reverend Mornuff from The Bronx. Was he the killer or just another John? Taking nothing for granted, they'd follow him just to make sure. Sure, there is an element of the 'Savior' in the type of killings discovered here and on Long Island – which could mean, that maybe he wanted to take these women off the street, but they denied him, thus bringing out the very worst in him, to make him want to at least save their souls from farther chastisement from G'd!

They followed the Caddy up to the Bronx, where he drove into the parking lot of the Church. Escorting the lady in the back door of the church, they sat and waited for an hour or more. When the two of them emerged from the church, they then knew he might not be who they were looking for, but they would still follow him until he'd return the lady to the Hell's Kitchen location. When he had done just that, they knew he was not their man.

So, the waiting game began again for the two of them. Looking across the street for that stunning lady of the night; Lopez didn't see any sign of her – he'd wonder if she tired of waiting and walked off, or got picked up by some John. The two of them would sit for the remaining night watching and following suspicious cars. Yes, this night was a bust – no ladies of the night killed or missing from this area. A successful night they thought, but when they returned to the Precinct later that morning; they heard about a male body being found not too far from Hell's Kitchen area. Thinking nothing much about it, the two of them signed out and went home.

THE AUTOPSY

Chief of Police Notting: "So, what have you found to be the cause of death Doc!"

In the City Morgue awaiting the report on the dead John Doe – Chief Notting and Captain Wise waited outside the examination room. Finger prints had just been taken, and were sent uptown via email for identification of the 'Vic'. Coming out to greet them was Medical Examiner Sing;

who'd been on the job for too long, and was about to retire.

ME Sing: "You men made it here just in time. We just finished removing body evidence and washing it for examination and autopsy. Come on in and take a smock and face cover before we start. I just want you to know, that there seems to be some similar occurrence, with death and no signs of cause. Just on observation when he came in, was, that his eyes were not dilated – like sudden death overcame him. Come in and sit down – if you want coffee, there's some in the office – let's began will we!"

Looking over the entire body for a second time – not noticing any wounds of any type; checking the mouth for broken teeth, the hands for defensive wounds and once again the eyes, which were not dilated. After he took up the scalpel and made his first incisions. From the navel to the throat and, then across from one nipple to the other. Opening up the chest cavity to expose the internal organs; a gasp was heard from the assistance.

ME Sing: "Yes, I know! This makes number three! Come and get a closer look Chief Notting. Here you will notice that the insides are dried up and still intact."

Chief Notting: "Yes, I see but, what is the cause? Are there any drugs in his system that might cause this to occur? And if not drugs; was he kept in a closet or something like that, to have his insides dry up like that? What is your best explanation Doctor?"

MI Sing: "Well, as of this moment, I have no explanation to offer you. But one thing I can attest to is that, it is the same person involved in this killing that is with the other two. Here, look at the abrasions on their penis – the same as these photos here. It's like they used the same tool to inflict punishment before killing their victims. You find MI this tool, and I'll testify to his involvements in these three deaths."

Chief Notting: "Okay with the penis test; but what about the internal organs being dried up and the skin outside is soft to the touch. So, tell MI Doctor what's going on here, if you know?"

ME Sing: "Too much to think about now – just find out who this guy is, and maybe you'll find someone or something to put together with these three murders."

Removing the smocks, Chief Notting and his Captain Wise huddled together in a corner. It was then that Captain Wise's cell phone rang.

Captain Wise: "Okay I got it; now, get Detectives Lopez and Lake to get on this matter. I and Chief Notting will gather the other information from the ME concerning the two other men. Yes, I understand they just got off their shift, I need them back on this case – there seems to be a connection with this and the murdered street women.*

Okay; bye! Chief; there may be a group of 'vigilantes' out there making up for the murder of the women. I put Lopez and Lakes on this to cover both sides of this matter. Now, let's inform the family now that his identity is confirmed!"

Chief Notting: "Send someone from the station to do that, it's not my job to do such things."

Captain Wise: "It's the Mayors son Rick! I thought he looked familiar on that table. I don't want the Media getting there before we do sir. You know how they pickup information via leaks within the department. We can be there in ten minutes – we'll drive up the FDR (parkway in Manhattan) to the Gracie Mansion."

Detective Mary Lake: "Yes Lopez; I got the call a few minutes ago. I'll come get you at your home in fifteen minutes. Where are we going to first... ohh! Okay, I'll bring a extra set of pants." They were going to the Morgue and Mary had a soft stomach for certain things, and viewing dead bodies was one of them.

She picked Lopez up at his home and they drove downtown to the morgue. Arriving at the morgue, both Lake and Lopez entered and went straight to ME Sing office for any updates on the bodies. Entering his office, they found him looking through a pile of books on his desk, that he didn't see the two of them come in.

ME Sign: "Oh, I didn't notice you standing there; here, come in and find a set – I want to look at one more thing here."

Pulling up two chairs to the front of his desk, Lake and Lopez sat and waited for him to finish reading from the open books.

ME Sign: "There is something very peculiar about the internal organs of the three men in there, which might have an explanation. I was looking for some reason why their organs might've dried from within the body. I thought, maybe there is a machine that inserted through the throat and a type of dry ice material is injected – but, that is not so, because there is no toxicity in their blood – so, I thought maybe being placed in a decompression chamber for hours; but that didn't make any sense either, because the eyes would at least be dilated and they're not. I was mystified until I opened this book. Now, don't go jumping off the cliff when I show you. I just want you to have an open mind and then decide what to think. Here; this book say (Dr. Sign had a witchcraft book in his hand) that, it is either 'Voodoo' or 'Witchcraft' behind this matter. Here it says; that a spell can be placed upon the living and drain out their sprites to be consumed the 'High Priest' to preserve their longevity on Earth. But, it also says, that this spell was only used to keep safe the wrongfully dead."

Detective Lake: "You mean to say; that someone who is either dead or alive was killed wrongfully be someone, and that they the dead, seeks out the living and does, what exactly Doctor?"

ME Sign: "It says that it is for reestablishing life to the dead so it may ascend with its soul to the heavens!"

Detective Lopez: "Now, that sound like 'bullshit' if I've never heard it before. Dead people walking around looking for live humans to suck out their souls. Now; what are we looking for on the streets, a Voodoo slave with wide eyes and dirty face and clothes? Give us an idea of what to look for Doctor Sing!"

ME Sing: "Not sure what they look like; but, you will know once you're in the present of such evil. Just let me say this. There will be more killing of this type until you find them and eliminate them – how many they may be."

Detective Lake: "And how do you suppose we do that? How can you kill the dead if they're already dead Doctor? Are they to be burned on the stake like in Salem Massachusetts? This is farfetched for sure!"

Detective Lopez: "Thank you anyway Doctor Sing; we'll take it from here, and please keep us updated if another body shows up. We have other investigations to pursue. We have a serial killer out there killing women, and now we see these women maybe taking matters into their hands also."

Taking in perspective what had been revealed to them; they walked out got into the car and sat. They need time to mull over what just transpired in the Morgue. Putting the key into the ignition and turning on the car; Mary Lake had much to say.

Detective Lake: "I'm trying to put my finger on this – first, we have the killing of the Prostitute here and on Long Island – and now we have Johns being targeted by; what, Voodoo devils who suck out the souls of these men. No, this is too much for me to fathom."

Detective Lopez: "I ain't buying this bullshit for one second. There's someone out there with a new drug, which causes these affects. I say we concentrate on finding the serial killer, and hopefully we'll come across the killer of these three men. It's academic my lady Watson – now, let's go get something for breakfast."

ANGEL OF BEAUTY

John: "Oh my goodness; I must say baby – you are the most beautifully whore that I have ever had the pleasure – tell, me what you want and how much!"

Terri: "What's your name honey? You're a piece of cheese yourself honey! I'll do whatever you want and the price is whatever you will give me. Just take me to the 'Gay White Way' and then we'll spend the rest of the night lying in each other's arms."

John: "No, I'm not Gay at all. My name is Thomson Toms. I straight as an arrow baby, but we can hang out together. You have some very funny dictums with you."

Aware of her speech style not being as his; she noted that all the others would have to acquaint themselves with the speech patterns of today.

Terri: "I want to go now Mr. Toms; if you are ready. I will show you where to drive where we can park and make out.

Getting into the car, they drove up Broadway towards Harlem, where she would direct him to then drive towards the river. There they would bring the car to a stop and sit inside while making out. After a few minutes of touching; she suggested they go sit on the bench under the tree.

Waleed Yaser

Terri: "Come on honey sit with me here. The car's too small for what I want to do with you. If you have a blanket in the bonnet we can lay under instead."

John: "Yes, I have a blanket in the trunk – you're not from England are you; because, you said bonnet instead of trunk – but anyway yes I have one."

Spreading the blanket out underneath the tree; they laid down and begun kissing. She stuck her tongue deep into his mouth, and began breathing in. His eyes grew very large and his hands dropped to his side. He was now in a state of limbo, unable to talk or move. She stood up and walked over beyond the tree and lifted up a very large manhole cover with one hand. She dragged his body over and slowly descended with his body into the hole. She then emerged again and walked over to his car, put it in gear and let it go down the hill where it went over a Clift and down into the river and sank to the bottom. Walking back to the hole, she took the manhole cover and disappeared within.

Down in the hole we see her dragging the body down a few steps which led to a pool of water; where she then took his body and went under water. His body was buoyant but hers was not, as she walked down the corridor where at the end a light could be seen. Coming up as the light grew larger she walked up eight steps into a room. In the room stood the other women who all awaited her arrival.

Lady Rue: "Give him to Staci to finish her revival – that will make four of my girls back – and nine more girls to go, before I can revive myself. What did you learned today Terri, that we can use on the outside?"

Terri: "Our speech is from our time. Though I can understand them, we will have to listen more to learn their words of today. The year is now; 2010 month of August. We must remember to use the words of today."

Ms. Rue: "That is good Terri! Who will go out next and bring us a new body! Cynthia or Denise will have to go, until Staci is stronger to go out in the world. Whoever goes out; take the body with you and leave it where it could be found."

Cynthia: "I will go out next Lady Rue! I will take the body out later tonight and make ready for tomorrow. I will speak with Terri about what not to say out there. We must keep our location secret until we all are revived again."

Looking around the room; we see Lady Rue, whose face and body is dry rotted, her hair patchy and gray and her clothing torn and decaying with mold spots. All the remaining women were in the same state of decaying, rotten bodies. Staci was hovering over the body before sticking her mouth onto his mouth; and began sucking out his soul and sprite. Her eyes brighten up when she was finish removing his soul. She then took his body and placed it before the exit, where it would later be taken out and disposed of. They all stood around not saying anything, but just looking at each other. In their eyes; they were all very beautiful women. Who happen to be trapped in this dwelling with only one way out, and that was to kill the family member of those who'd placed them in this predicament in the first place.

Much later in the enclave; Cynthia broke away from the circle and took up the body in her hand. Walking down the steps into the water, she walked under the water, which seemed to change her appearance from a rotting body, to that of a beautiful well dressed woman. Coming up on the other side she placed the body down and climbed up and removed the manhole cover. Peering out to make sure no one was around; she retrieved the body and carried his as though he was drunk. Walking down a poorly lit street; she found a doorstep that went down three steps and left him near the garbage cans. Walking back to the park, she removed the manhole cover and climbed inside; where she began the walk back underwater to their enclave.

Mercedes: "Uhhhh! Can you feel life leaving your body bitch! I guess you are now wishing you'd changed your lifestyle right? Feel my hand tightening around your throat as you look for a breath but none is there; so, just give up the ghost bitch – I need more satisfaction tonight after I'm finish with you, so die!"   He had moved to Hunt's Point for this victim and was not satisfied, because of the low standard these girls carried. Not really the sophisticated type of women he was used to killing – these were low class for sure – not even worth his stopping but he had the itch, which he had to be scratched. He would drop her along the road somewhere and head towards Hell's Kitchen where the pickings were much prettier.

Detective Lopez: "Mary wake up! Listen, it's getting late – the sun about to rise anytime now so let's pack it in for the night. We'll get an early start tomorrow night."

Detective Lake: "Yawn! That sounds good to me, because this car is not right for sleeping. I just can't get comfortable – next time we take my car, it has more foot room." Just then; a radio call came in and Lake answered it. "Yes sir I understand. Two more bodies – one found in Harlem and the other by Jerome Avenue in the Bronx. We're heading right over there sir – over and out!"

Detective Lopez: "Looks like we're not going home as planned. Let's hit the Harlem location first, its close by!"

Detective Lake: "Sure why not; the Captain says one of the bodies, is surely related to our case. It's a woman in her late twenties who'd been strangled. As for the other, we'll have to make that determination ourselves.

Driving with sirens wailing and flashing lights, they arrived at the Harlem location in five minute. Exiting the car, both Lake and Lopez listened to the I witness account of the body being dropped off.

Witness: "I heard this funny sound out front and walked to the window to see what it was. I only saw what looked to be a shape of a woman; but I can't be sure but it looked female. Well, when I looked down I saw a body laying there and first thought he'd fallen asleep or was drunk and fell down or just found a place to sleep it off. I really didn't think too much of it, until, I came back to the window and saw that he hadn't even moved to get into a better resting posistion. So, I got my gun and walked down to wake him up – didn't know if he'd be violent, so just to be safe I took it. First I tried to wake him by yelling to him that he should leave before I call a cop. He didn't move so, took a broom stick and poke him two or three times, and when he didn't move then, I walked down and shook him. And, that is when he fell over onto his back. And, now here you people are."

Detective Lake: "Don't worry sir; we'll take it from here! You can go back inside; a officer will come write down your explanation for our records. As for that gun; you do have a permit to own it right?"

Witness: "Sure do Detective! I'll go get it; it's in my drawer where I keep my gun also!"

Detective Lopez: "No problem sir; we just had to ask! We'll be leaving now, and the people from the morgue will come pick up the body. Thank you again sir!"

Detective Lake: "Okay; let's go take a quick look at the body in the Bronx, and then take me home so I can sleep. I'm out on my feet and I don't know if I can make it beyond the next hour."

Mama Bolognese: "Vincent wake up! Wake up you lazy ass good for nothing son of mines. I asked you to watch over the restaurant a few nights a week and you can't even do that. Where were you last night until dawn? I heard you drive up and saw the sun coming up from the window. The maitre d at the restaurant, said that you never showed up to work and that he had to pull a double shift. This has got to stop and you've got to take more responsibility with your life. You didn't want to work with your father in the family business, so, we sent you to college and there all you did was party. Five years of school and still you won't work in your profession. What, Wall Street money is no good for you also. My patience is

31

running thin with you. Now, get your head right or find a place where you can do nothing. Now, get up and clean this room!"

Mama Bolognese had come from the Main House to the Pool House, where Vincent lived away from the rest of the family. He abhorred the type of Mafia life style he'd grew up with, and never wanted to be a part of it.

Vinnie: 'I have no peace in this house. Between Mama and Uncle Vito – it's either work trafficking in drugs or sweeping up the spilled pasta. I know what I want in life, and that's to become the worst serial killer who ever lived. If I can go on for the next ten years killing once or twice a month, I'll be a legend that all will speak about and even write many books about. Nobody cares about whores anyway, so what if their dead – I'm ridding the world of filth anyway! Tonight I'll take off and spend it at the restaurant, so I can get uncle and mom off my back.

A NEW MOON

A new night begins with a much darker evening before us. The new Moon was just beginning, and the stars were covered by clouds, thus, darkness prevailed. All along the strip walked ladies of the night. Vehicles of all kinds drove slowly up Eighth Avenue as they sampled the wares to purchase. *It was a very warm muggy night, so the ladies were even scantier dressed. Men would vie for the most beautiful, well equipped (big tits, and plump ass) woman on the block. Some were classily dressed and got only certain responses from the Johns in their cars.*

Parked well down the street next to a boarded up store front; so they almost sat cloaked under the darkness of the night. Detective Lake and Lopez were back on watch for the 'Strangler' who had struck only a few days ago in the Bronx. The body of the man found was now the forth one found with his inners sucked dry. Now, they were connecting the two deaths as one but with two killers. All involved Johns; of whom, all had arrest records with solicitation of prostitution. As they were now working a double case which normally meant; lots of overtime and intensive investigation.

As the normal going about on the street increased; with Johns walking and driving about the area. They both realized that they had too much on their hands, and that they would need to implement a decoy type of investigating. But, how many women would be needed here and downtown by Thirty First Street near Tenth Avenue.

Across from where they parked; a crowd was growing amongst what looked to be one woman. It was normal for this to happen, when one man sought to out bid another for her services. Walking over to see what was going on; Lopez stood on the outer edge of the crowd. Noting that it was three men arguing with each other – one being a known Pimp; who's problem was that she was not one of his girls, and that she should not be here on the corner in the first place, until she gets in with his stall of women.

Lowdown: "You've got no right being a lone mare on my streets. You either come into my fold or get off this street. This money is mines and on one gets any of it unless I give approval."

Cynthia: "I have my Madam who I work for and these streets don't belong to you or anyone like you. I will give my twath to whoever has the most money."

Lowdown: "You've got such a mouth on you bitch. Let's say I smack you around a little, that'll teach you to respect who's in charge around here."

Cynthia: "You try that and I'll cut you from one ear to the other!" She reached under her dress and pulled a razor (pearl handle) from her garter belt. A stylish razor the like of which; have not been seen in years. "Move on and get your milk maids elsewhere."

Lowdown: "Oh! You're a little rough bitch with balls uh! No problem now, but you will join my stable whether you like it or not." Walking away and crossing the street to stand in his normal viewing vantage point, he monitored the happenings on the street. He would plan something special for her at his discretion.

Walking back across the street; Lopez entered the car and told Detective Lake about how the Pimp got served his own medicine by a petite pretty woman. He told her about the razor she drew on him and forced him to retreat back to his hole.

For the next few hours, the business on the street went about as normal. It was a busy night as woman and John did their business – some in the back of cars as well as behind doors to apartment buildings. Even the local bar served as a place of pleasure – as long as the owner got his dibs.

Sitting in the car watching all the activities, both Lake and Lopez talked about their love life and their favorite dish to cook. Every now and then, Lopez would get out and walk along the street, listening to what deals were being made and what disappointment a John felt when his price was too little. Getting back to the car he would sit watching as Lake would take a short nap; who would then wake and allow Lopez to catch a few zzzzz's!

It was getting near dawn, when a radio call came in from headquarters. It was another John, whose body was still on sight. The body was sitting on a bench in a park on Saint Nicholas Avenue. When they arrived at the park, the do not cross tape kept the uniform officers back, until a detective got on the scene. Walking up to the body; both Lake and Lopez notice the same facial response like that seen on the other four. If things went as they have for the past few days; a dead prostitute would be found before the sun rose. But this time it would not occur as they thought. There would be no prostitute to place on the story board back at headquarters. There were now five Johns, which conveyed the presents of a 'serial killer' amongst them.

Detective Lopez: "Now do you believe there's another serial killer out there. It has to be a woman doing this, but how could she do it alone if she had to move the body. She's having other prostitute to work with her – plus, look at the face; he's smiling a little – and nothing puts a smile on a man's face, but a woman.

Detective Lake: "Well; I guest one must go undercover to weed out the woman or women involved. We'll need about three girls to be our eyes and ears. I know four new officers who'd pass for street walkers. I'll speak with them later this morning at headquarters when the shift changes. I'd dress up myself if I wasn't so thick in the hips…. Lol lol !"

Detective Lopez: "Yeah, I'd like to see you dressed up in something tight and sassy! You'd look real good! Lol lol!"

Ms. Rue: *"Eight more men is needed to revive us all, so we may walk amongst the living again. Our mission is to find the family members of Salami, Pasta and Bolognese before we are allowed to transcend to the next world. Always ask these men, their names and never go with anyone but white men. That is where we will find our salvation to the hereafter. Whose time is it tonight to go out?"*

Denise: *"It is my time Madam Rue; I will listen out for any of these names and that Pimp who wants to derail our mission. Should I take his life if he interferes with me tonight?"*

Ms. Rue: *"Kill him if you can do it without being seen. Consume his body and then place him in a trash can. We don't need distractions when we have purpose for living the lost life taken from us. We need these men so let us not scare them away by being to 'High Brow' – make the prices easy for them. Charge no more than fifty dollars for each man. It is almost time for you to leave Denise. Let us all pray for our dead souls!"*

Walking through the water as the light of death causes the water to glow, Denise comes up on the other side beautiful; dressed in a lime green silk dress which comes to her ankles. Ascending to the street; she looks about before leaving the manhole. As she walks down the street she tried earnestly to smell the air, but could only smell the last smell they all smelt when death over took the whole of them.

The night was breeze as she could feel her dress brushing up against her legs. Even the breeze across her face had her needing even more to be alive again. All these years asleep to be waken and thrust into a world unbeknownst to her and the others, only made this mission of finding the family responsible for their death a necessity. She had been walking down Eight Avenue for awhile, when she saw the masses already gathering. She walked amongst them and found her place near a restaurant alley way. There she stood propped up against the side of the building, watching the men pass by while examining her body. She would pull up her dress higher above her knees; attracting the eyes of many who passed by. Out of all the other women on the street, she was surely one of the most beautiful – but as for all the other girls in Ms. Rue's brothel, she was maybe the fifth most beautiful among them.

Streetwalker: "Hey girlfriend; what you got that's attracting all these men? I've been out here for two hours now, and I haven't got as many propositions as you have and, you just got here. What'd say I just stand over here and catch a few strays walker by?"

With an impassive look upon her face; she waved the hooker on her way. She didn't need anyone to hamper her quest of attracting the right kind of men. With both of them Negro's she knew only other of their kind would gather around them.

Denise: "No; please do not stand next to me! I work alone tonight; you will attract more Negro men to me, when I only need white men to date me. Now please go okay!"

Streetwalker: "Well I say! No need to get all puffed out with pride – like you some special black girl – but to be called a Negro; well that takes the cake! I haven't heard that word in a very long time. Where you come from girlfriend the south? I thought you people evolved down there or are you still stuck in being maids for whitey? Don't worry I'm leaving – maybe you need to grow up and get some culture about yourself." Walking off into the night; leaving Denise standing alone waiting for any white man to offer her a date.

Johns: "Hey girl; you wantta party with the three of us!" Standing before her, were three white men in their early thirty's. They were obviously drunk and horny for pussy. There before them was Denise, who was eager to take these three on. Three at one time was something she could handle.

Denise: "It will cost you dearly for taking on three of you. But, I am sure that you have enough to pay for this date right? Here; follow me to where we can be alone and not bothered. It is a short walk to the park!"

Johns: "No need to walk girl; we have a car over there. We can ride – which way are we heading?"

Denise: "Head uptown towards Riverside Drive. There is a park where we can roll in the grass and enjoy good sex. I will even allow all three of you to do me at once."

Streetwalker: "There is nothing really to report now Detective Lake." Detective Lake was undercover as she stood near one of the unmarked cars. She had a earpiece in to listen to the broadcast, in case something went down, where she had to respond quickly. "There was this one thing I found funny; it's this girl dressed in a pretty silk dress, who used words that haven't been used in years. I was thinking she was from the South; but, knowing how they have evolved when it comes to race relationship, that maybe she was from some other place. She is standing over there! Oh, where did she go so quickly? Anyway, I just thought she was somewhat peculiar. Other than that, there is nothing to report. The other girls are walking about keeping an eye out for the 'Strangler'!"

Detective Lake: "That is good; you can take a message to the other girls, to be attentive to what's going on around them. It has been two days now, and the Strangler has not returned to the streets. It could be that we have *frightened him to stay off the streets or he's moved to another local. Anyway stay on point and try and stay in sight. Do not get into any car unless you signal one of the tag team cars." Sending her off into the night; Mary Lake began her walk about also.*

Denise: "There's the park over there. You can park near the bench and we'll walk to the bushes and lay on the grass."

Johns: "We have a blanket to spread on the ground honey. I'll get it and we can have a picnic tonight; all were going to eat is you for dinner!"

Walking over to the darkest area in the park, they laid on the ground and all hands went to different areas on her body. She laid there for a few moments and one by one kissed them. The first one fell back on the blanket. The second one fell onto her lap, as the third one sat on his knees frozen still with an austere look on his face. One by one she would lower them down into the hole. Once all three were down, she took them by their leg and took them into the water to the room where the others waited.

Ms. Rue: "Very nice Denise! Three at one time; Blanch, Ada and Mary take them to revive yourselves then come and join us in the circle to pray.

The three women took up the men and stuck their tongues into their mouths. A glow began to emit from the three of them, as they retrieved the souls from each of the men bodies. They then returned to the circle and prayed for the life which was taken from them and for the continuous curse upon the families until vengeance is done.

Ms. Rue: "Now, you three remove the bodies – disperse them throughout the city and then return home."

Denise: "No, do not take then in this manner – but, take them and return them to the car parked at the end of the park. It is a white four door car – if you look in the pockets you will find keys. I noticed how they turn the car on; so, I will go with you and place them in the car and start it. I will then make the car drive down the street until it crash and comes to a stop. That is how we will dispose of these three."

Ms. Rue: "This is good Denise. We have to all learn the new way of these people. I hope to soon go out from here and see what the world has become. I cannot leave until all of you are revived first. Tomorrow we will send out three girls to hasten our revival. Blanch; Ada and Mary are going out to bring back three men. So, go and dispose of the bodies and return to pray for our souls."

Mercedes: 'Stank bitches; nothing but stank bitches here.' Driving along the lower Westside around Twentieth Street and Tenth Avenue; while looking for a victim his hunger for death had overcome him, and he wanted to feed himself. There was nothing special about these types of women, so, a different location was necessary, before he'd lose his mind and do something really stupid. 'I should've just stayed in Howard Beach, and found someone there at a bar; but, shitting in your own backyard is not good for the family. Anyway, I'm here in Manhattan so; better make the best of it. I'll drive up to Chelsea first and if I don't find anything there, then I'll head to Hell's Kitchen and check out the women there.'

Driving up the Westside Highway; he drove by a 'Strip Club' and decided to stop and check out the wears within. Parking his car at a parking lot and walking into the strip club; he found what could feed his hunger for this evening. There on stage danced a blonde who flung herself around a poll. She would prance about and temp the many men sitting at the bar for tips for a shake of her tits in their faces. Richard sat drinking his rum and coke while placing dollar bills in her bra and thong – while sizing her up for what he needed to do before the night was out.

Mercedes: "HEY GIRL WHAT OTHER DANCE CAN YOU DO FOR ME!" The music made it hard for him to convey his real needs. So he motioned to her to meet him in the private room, as he dropped a hundred dollar bill before her feet.

Waleed Yaser

Entering one of the private rooms; he sat in the chair and summoned the waiter to come. He would have a bottle of wine brought and chilled as he waited for the girl to finish her time on stage.

Lady Hustler: "Hey baby; thank you for the invite. I need to explain something before we get started. For this hundred dollar bill that you laid at my feet, it will only get you a lap dance of twenty minutes. Now, for even more of my time it will depend on what you are willing to pay. So tell me sweetheart; what are you looking for me to do?"

Mercedes: "I'm looking to spend on you blonde nothing less than two grand for a all nighter." Throwing a wad of cash onto the table before him, he motioned for her to sit and pour the wine. "I have a penthouse on Central Park west – so, we can finish this bottle and leave for my place if you want. Tell me what you think blonde?"

Lady Hustler: "Anything you can pay for should be yours to have." Grabbing the wad of cash and counting it, she sat on his lap and poured him a drink. "I'm not due to dance anymore tonight, so, if you want we can leave after this bottle is emptied."

Mercedes: "My name is Richie; what's yours blonde?"

Lady Hustler: "Toni honey; nice to meet you!" Though she was in the present of the devil himself, her fate was written and the ink is dry!

Walking out the strip club and up the block to where he parked the car. The back of his neck began to sweat profusely from the anticipation of his victim. As they drove up Eighth Avenue towards his suppose penthouse. He suddenly pulled off the street and onto the entry of Central Park. The entry was blocked by a barrier but he maneuvered around and headed to the under path towards the Eastside.

Lady Hustler: "Slow down baby, you're going to crash for sure and mess up your Mercedes. Where are you going now – your place is on the other side right?"

Not saying a word, until he was well into the tunnel – he brought the car to a stop!

Mercedes: "You are in the presents of a Serial Killer; and now I have to kill you!" Grabbing her around the neck, he pushed her head down towards the floor mat. Holding her there while looking out the window for approaching cars, his grip soon forced the fighting woman to cease – she had let go of her ghost. He pushed her body to the floor and continued to the end of the tunnel. Looking about for anyone coming; he opened the passenger door and pushed her out and drove around the other barrier, and sped away quickly. She would lay there behind the barrier for almost an hour, before a passing patrol car came and noticed her laying there.

Streetwalkers: *"We're reporting in for final orders Detective Lake. Nothing has transpired since our last convergence two hours ago. We all have nothing to speak of but, that we're very tired of walking up and down all night. Can we pack it in for tonight and try again tomorrow?"*

Detective Lake: *"Yes, I don't see why not. I'll signal everyone to stand down – and bring Detective Lopez down from the roof, where he's been doing reconnaissance duties for you girls safety. You three can walk around the corner, and I'll have one of the safe cars to pick you up. I'll wait for Lopez to come down and we'll meet everybody at the station."*

Getting back into the car as she waited for Lopez; she turned on the radio to listen to some music. It was a little past 3 a.m. when the passenger door open and in got Lopez.

Detective Lopez: *"There's no good place to sit up there – almost feel asleep a couple of times – plus, there's nothing really to look at from that vantage point. I can really only see certain parts of the street. What happens underneath me is out of my view, so, next time we will have to have another man on the opposite side to make sure we cover everything."*

Back at the Station House before the next shift was to start; both Lake and Lopez were in the back catching up on lost sleep. They were awaken by one of the detectives who was assigned to the case, that another body was found earlier that morning, and that they needed to go investigate. They gathered up their gear and drove to the Eastside entrance to Central Park. There they saw up to five CSI agents working the scene.

Lopez: "Hey fellows what's going on? You people got anything for me to go on?"

CSI: "Nothing really; except a slight trace of tire tracks – which we are trying to enhance to photo. Seems like she was dropped from a car here – so, we have a team on the other end looking to see if they can locate some tire tracks of this kind with more imagery to match what we have here. It's not going to be easy but, we'll get something to you by the end of the day. As for any trace evidence; we've found nothing out of the ordinary."

Lake: "She had no identification on her person when she was found? She looks like she a worker but not the street type. Maybe she's an exotic dancer or private dancer. Have her finger prints send over asap to be identified – if she did work on the inside, she'd have to be registered by the business. Come Lopez; let's head down to the Morgue. I want to see for myself if she's another victim of our serial killer. And here we've spent all night on the street and he's gone inside to snatch up another trophy."

ALL IN ONE NIGHT!

ME: "Good thing you two got here early to view three examinations. They all seem to be from the same killer. With the exception of the abrasion which seem to be done by different individuals. It's like whatever vagina did this was dry or sandy. It's hard to put my hands around the explanation."

Detective Lopez: "Don't go getting crazy on me Doctor. So you might be saying that these women or woman, are either dried up dead sex or they're using sandpaper? This is getting a bit too much for my thought process to calculate. But, we didn't come down here about three men – we came about the woman found just off the park. It is a strangling that brings us here – we'll take a look at the other three before we leave. Now, show us the girl!"

ME: "Sure no problem; just thought you wanted to know! You know, having two or more Serial Killers working the streets at the same time smells of complicity which means it is likely to be a gang or sorts; now, that's just my conclusion!"

It was during the autopsy, that trace evidence was found in her hair. These items were then taken back to CSI at 1 Federal Plaza, for analyzing and identification. Detectives Lake and Lopez waited for over four hours for the findings. That had given them the time to sleep, before heading back out for an all nighters on the streets.

CSI: "Okay you two; I've got something for you to go on."

Waking up from sleeping in the plush chairs – both Lopez and Lake sat up looking blurry at the presentation held before them. Was this going to be their smoking gun – which would bring them to the doorstep of the 'Strangler'; or was it just a piece to the puzzle, that needed fitting into the right places?

CSI: "What I have here is an item taken from the hair of the victim – if you notice it is black and somewhat stringy – almost artificial, like carpet fibers. Well, when we did the analysis and complied the product with our database, we found that, it comes out of an Mercedes type vehicle. So, what you're looking for is a black interior car. As for the exterior of the car – it could either be any color but white. Most white vehicle will have either gray to lighter color interiors. You find me the car with the black carpet, and I will match the grade for you. If you guys come up with some other evidences just forward it to us and we'll help you get your man."

Waleed Yaser

Leaving Central Headquarters; Lake and Lopez drove up town to their station house on the Westside.

Detective Lake: "Just drop me at my place so I can get a different dress for this evening, before the second shift starts. We're going to have the same crew as last night, so, we need to make sure they have the newest information we have. At least they'll know we'll be looking for a Mercedes with one man inside. He's going to slip up one night and we're going to pounce upon him like a Gorilla on a banana!"

Detective Lopez: "Yeah; he's going to get lazy and not watch his own back. It seems he got a bit sloppy with this young lady. I'm sure he didn't expect she'd be registered and traceable with just a fingerprint. Hopefully when we get to the precinct they'll have her information ready for us to start tracking this guy down.

The drive to Lakes apartment on the upper Eastside took only ten minutes and almost thirty minutes for her to pick out a dress for undercover work tonight. When she came out the apartment building, and got into the car; Lopez stared at her with disgust.

Detective Lake: "What! What's the problem with you?"

Detective Lopez: "Thirty minutes to get one dress; it takes you that long just to get one dress? You could've purchased one from a Boutique in less time. You know how I hate waiting for women to do anything like getting clothes and stuff."

Detective Lake: "Clam down Lopez; it's just that I couldn't find the right shoes to go with this dress – you know I have to look the part, otherwise it's not realistic – and we want realism when we go undercover right? Now, drive the car and keep quiet!"

MY MISTAKE

It was getting near 8 p.m. when the second shift was to begin. Captain Wise stood before the crowd of officers, detectives and administration (desk officers) who, was about to tell of them of the coming evenings priorities. Sitting in the back of the room, chatting with the three undercover girls about what to look for this evening Lake and Lopez made it clear not to let their guard down. A hard knock upon the front desk said of the attention now directed to the Captain.

Captain Wise: "Okay listen up People! Tonight we're going to hit the streets and make the streets safe for our citizens. I want Time Square to the River safe for the foreigners coming from the Ocean Liners. I want everyone to pay attention and get home safely tonight. You two in the back; Lake and Lopez! Stay around after we dismiss from duty call. I need to know where you two are in the investigation. Okay; everyone is dismissed from quarters!" As the room was empting out, the Captain walked towards the back of the room, to speak with both Lake and Lopez.

Captain Wise: "Okay you two; tell me where you're at and how close are we to finding the killers – how many are there now; six I was told is the number now – get to getting this case closed. The Mayor is breathing down the Chief's back for closure of his son's death. How many more men and women have be laid out in the morgue, before we get these people? I need results in this case people – now, tell me where you're at!"

Lopez: "We have decoys out there, and Detective Lake has even put herself undercover in trying to solve case sir. We have the whole block monitored with search cars that go out following suspicious Johns when they pick up a client. So far, we have tailed over fifteen cars, and nothing has happen but the normal things. Plus now we have an idea of what he might be driving. The last lady found on Central Park East, had trace evidence of carpet fibers and they been identified as coming from a Mercedes vehicle. So, now we're concentrating on all Mercedes that will come into the area. We should have him within a week or two at the most. He's already slipped up once by leaving trace evidence, now we have to wait and see if he gets sloppy so we can pounce on him."

Captain Wise: "Do whatever you have to and get this thing closed! Now, get out there and be safe." He then walked off into the command center and disappeared into the vast crowd of officers.

Detective Lake: "I'll go get dressed now. We'll meet downstairs at the car; or if you want, you and the decoy cars can go and setup and I'll bring the girls."

Detective Lopez: "Okay; we'll meet you girls over there – give us about half an hour to setup and get in position. I got a feeling we're going to make contact tonight with the 'Strangler' – if so, he's going down hard."

It was going on 9:45 p.m. when Detective Lake and the girls arrived. The night was warm and humid busy as usual. The street walkers went about their work, as did Lowdown watching over everything on his street. Detective Lake directed the ladies to move about and not to take tricks while on the street. And, they were to notify her when they were getting into a car with a John. Each decoy had their microphone and earplug for communication.

Hours had passed and nothing out of the norm had taken place. Detective Lopez was up on the roof watching the flow of women and Johns go about their business. It was then, that something caught his eye. There standing next to a light pole just opposite the bar, stood a women he thought he knew. He radioed to Lake that he wanted to investigate a hunch and that he'd get back in position afterwards.

Walking down the stairway to the ground floor; all he could think about is whether this girl was one of his schoolmates he once dated while living in the Bronx. Walking out onto the sidewalk, he slowly made his way to the woman, who'd been in conversation with a prospective John. When he saw she was not interested, he walked up and spoke to her.

Detective Lopez: "Hey baby can I ask you a question?" Touching her on the shoulder to make her turn around he realized that it wasn't who he thought it was; but she surely looked like her twin. "Oh; I'm sorry I thought you were someone else I knew from my past. I don't mean to bother you!"

Ada: "What's your name boyfriend?"

Detective Lopez: "Hector Lopez; and what's yours may I ask! You look so much like my former lover that I had to come and find out."

Ada: "Is that name Italian; Lopez?"

Detective Lopez: "No, it is Latino or Puerto Rican – my family has been here since the 50's in the Bronx."

Ada: "Not interested so walk on!" She turned her head and ignored him.

Detective Lopez: "Wait one minute honey; I was just trying to make small talk, you don't have to be a huffy about yourself; you don't really look that good in the first place." Touching her again on her shoulder – he got a response he didn't expect.

She reached under her dress and pulled out a razor and turned to Lopez with an evil look of death in her eyes. It was a pearl handle and very sharp; from the glistening shine on the blade.

Ada: "I told you I'm not interested; now don't bother me again!"

Detective Lopez: "Okay okay; I'm sorry to have bothered you. I'll leave okay!" He turned and walked back to the apartment building and went inside. As he was walking up the stairs, it dawn on him, that that razor was the same one held by that girl a few days ago. And, now she had it in her position. There must be a connection here; maybe this is a group of ladies who are working the streets picking up men to kill. But, none of the Johns were cut with a razor – something doesn't make sense here.

Waleed Yaser

Walking back down to the ground floor, he stepped onto the stoop and just watched her. She would turn down every Black, and Latino who asked her out – exactly what was she looking for – remembering that all the men in the morgue, were Anglo's, he felt in his guts, he was on to something. So, he stood there just watching who'd be her victim for the evening.

Streetwalker: "I have a Mercedes pulling up to the curb; it is a dark color late model four door. Wait; have the car ready to follow! Hello there sweetheart; what can I do for you tonight."

Detective Lake: "Okay; car one standby to follow Asia if she gets into the car. It may be the Mercedes that we're looking for, and if it is the Strangler; we don't want him to get out of our sight. If she gives me the signal to follow I'll give you the ok! Now, standby!" The word for a deal was Precious – she listened to every word being said within the car.

Voices in car: "So, first I must ask you this; are you a cop sweetheart?" "No, I'm no cop – now, tell me what you want me to do and, where's the money!" "Oh, I have the money sweetheart, but how much do you want and what will you do for the money." "I'll do whatever you ask of me – all we have to do is to go somewhere and get it done – I'm very busy tonight okay let's go precious!" "Anything you say sweetheart – here, how's this cash looks to you?"

"Nice baby nice! Two hundred will get you everything I have – drive down the street and turn at the next corner."

Detective Lake: "Okay car one get up behind her and do not lose her. Car two back him up but stay back! All other girls report back to me here at the car." Was this their final break in the case of the Strangler; or just another bust of a John?

Detective Lopez: 'Well; she doesn't really seem too eager to make money – but, she is paying too much attention on these Anglo boys. Okay, there goes another car pulling up to the curb – he's getting out to talk to her – he's not driving a Mercedes either; but he's very interested in getting her. Let me right down his plate number and description – about 5'9" and weighing about 210 with medium length hair. Okay; he's opening his door to take her – I need to follow them – get to your car boy in a hurry before you lose them. Shit; someone double parked next to me! The Liquor Store! "Hey in there; this car belongs to someone – you have to move it now!"

Man: "I'm shopping in here, why don't you give me a minute and I'll move it okay!"

Detective Lake: "Move it now or I'll have it impounded ass-hole! This is a Police matter!" Showing his badge the patron put down his items and ran out to move the car. Getting in and racing down the street hoping to get a glance as to where they turn; he'd lost them in the seconds it took to get his car. 'Shit; I hope he's not a victim – how would I explain to the Captain losing them and not using my backup! It's really stupid of you Hector; really just stupid!' Listening to the radio; he'd heard Lake had made a bust. Was it the Strangler! "Come in Lake this is Lopez; where is your location?"

Detective Lake: "We are two blocks over on Tenth Avenue and Fifty Seventh Street. We have a dark color Mercedes and the driver is under arrest."

Detective Lopez: "I'll be there in five minutes!" Not turning on his lights and siren, he drove around the corner and parked in the middle of the street. There he saw four or five patrol cars lights flashing and the Mercedes surrounded by ten or more officers. The driver was in handcuff and leaned over the top of the patrol car, being searched for weapons. "Lake! Is this our man or not?"

Detective Lake: "Not sure yet; but we will impound his car and take samples of the rug for analyzation to see if they match. He is going down to the station now. You want to come or go back on the streets. I pulled all the girls off for tonight – so, it's up to you to come or stay – whichever you do is alright with me. I'll be back at the station; these shoes are killing my feet!"

Back at One Federal Plaza; they had booked the John and waited for the analyzation of the carpet fibers. It took almost two hours for them to come back with the results. What results they came back with was not what both Lake and Lopez were expecting.

CSI: "Detective Lake and Lopez; this is not the Strangler you have in custody. The fibers are totally different than the ones we found in the victims hair. Your search is still pending, so, get back out there and hope for the luck of an Irish leprechaun."

Detective Lake: "Luck has nothing to do with catching this Strangler; it's more of fate, which his time is sure to run out soon, and we'll be there to arrest his ass. He doesn't know, we have the type of car he drives and evidence which will hang him. Nothing to worry about for now; we'll be putting in the long hours of undercover work; while he has only to go out and find another victim – which gives us the upper hand, because we're constantly on the job looking and staking out area's he might haven't yet visited. So, I'm going to write my report for tonight and then go home and get some rest."

Before the two of them could even walk out of the door; a CSI officer came to inform them about the discovery of three more Johns. They were scattered throughout the Westside area. One was found on Ninth Avenue and Sixth

Waleed Yaser

Street and two found together on Riverside Drive and Seventh Street. The bodies were all found in immediate areas, and not too far from the stakeout.

When the two of them arrived at the Morgue; Lopez went straight to the cooler to view the faces of the dead. He wanted to know, if the identity he had written down matched either of the victims. Lake followed behind him wondering why he was in such a hurry to view the bodies. Entering the cooler; Lopez pulled out his pad and opened it to the description of the John he'd saw last night.

Detective Lopez: "Hey! Come here and show me the three bodies that came in last night. Has the Doctor examined them yet?"

Asst.ME: "No, he hasn't done it as yet! He's been busy back in his office catching up on paper work. Do you want me to get him for you?"

Detective Lopez: "No, not yet; first show me the three bodies of the Anglo males. I want to see if one of them matches a description I had taken while on the stakeout. If one of them does match what I have written here, then we'll know who's involved in their murder. Where are they?"

Asst.ME: "Just over here in the refrigerator. They just came in no more than an hour ago. They are still in civilian clothes; I haven't had the time to change them into smocks yet." Opening up all three and pulling them out for viewing. The assistant ME stood back and let the police do their job.

Detective Lake: "You think we got something here Hector! Here let me see what you have written down." Mary took the notebook from his hands, as he uncovered all three bodies.

Detective Lopez: "No, not this one! This one neither! Oh, wait! ME hand me a tape measurer — he looks about 200 to 210 lbs right, hair medium length — is that written there Mary?"

Detective Lake: "Yes, 210 pounds and medium length hair and his height is about 5 feet 9 inches. What's his height, measure him!" With the tape measurer in his hands, he asked the ME to hold it at his head and he measured down to his feet.

Detective Lopez: "It's about 5 feet 8 inches — which could match my measurement give or take an inch. This has to be my guy! Everything is the same about him." Then it dawned on him! A flashback went throughout his thinking process. The first lady who pulled the pearl handle razor on Lowdown the Pimp; and the other girl pulling the same exact razor on me; this has to be the connection the two of them were hoping for. "I think I know who's been doing this to these Johns! And, if it's the two women that I know of; then there has to be more of them walking around somewhere. These two ladies wearing almost the same clothes, and carrying the same type of razor blade. I don't call this a coincident, I call it a match! We now know what to look for tomorrow night. Classy dress women in stylish hair dress of say, the late sixties. And wearing garter belts to hide their razors."

Detective Lake: "Well, if you're sure about this then, we have to set up tomorrow night with undercover cars only. They will troll about the streets looking for this type of woman...."

Detective Lopez: "And one more thing I remember her saying. That she wasn't interested in Black or Latino men, but strictly Anglo men only. And what we've seen here in the morgue is only Anglo men. Looks like we got half this case already closed now; all we need is to catch the Strangler and we can go back to normal or a semblance of it."

Detective Lake: "Okay; then how do we go about staking this out?"

Detective Lopez: "We can get six or eight men from the recruitment class, and put them out there walking up and down the streets. We will have decoy cars; say about four, which either of the decoys can use when they have a woman who matches this description. They will all have master keys to the cars. Well Mary Lake; tonight we catch the cat by its tail. Let's get back to the stationhouse and inform the Captain of our findings."

THE JIG IS UP!

That evening at the stationhouse; the Captain had just dismissed the roll call for that evening shift. He would go to the back and ask that Detectives Lake and Lopez, brief him again on what they planned to do.

Detective Lopez: "We're taking seven men from this graduating recruitment class, and having them dress sporty and walk about Hell's Kitchen trolling for women. But, not just your regular ordinary hooker, but, a certain stylish dress hooker. They have orders to go wherever they want. We have four decoy cars waiting to be used if we need them; and lookouts at every corner on rooftops. We want to know which direction they will be heading so we don't lose them like I lost her the other night."

Captain Wise: "You mean to tell me now, that, you had this girl in your grips and you let her get away and commit another murder. Is that what you're telling me now Detective Lopez?"

Detective Lopez: *"Well; something like that Captain! I was about to follow them, when a double parked car blocked me in, and by the time I got into the street, they had already disappeared from sight. Don't worry sir; we have this under control now that we know what to look for."*

Captain: *"Okay; then get to getting and bring me in some criminals to prosecute!"*

Mercedes: *'Nothing here on Flatbush Avenue worth doing; nothing even on Far Rockaway Boulevard and I need gas in the car. Let me gas up and then try Chinatown, they always got hot tiny women walking around. Yes; Chinatown it is going to be.'* *"Uh, please fill it up with Premium; thank you!"* *'Damn Mexican taking someone's job!'* *Making his way into Manhattan, would take him about one hour, due to traffic congestion on the Belt Parkway.*

When he arrived in Chinatown, he made a bee line to Mott Street and drove slowly up and down the tight well lit streets. He'd come up on these three ladies, hanging outside a restaurant and proposed something to them. Not getting the response he was looking for, he drove to another street and tried he best to recruit one of them into the car.

He would drive through Chinatown unsuccessful in his quest of scoring a chick. Fed up with the lack of prospects; he decided to head up town to area's he knew would afford him the picks of the litter. He didn't want to go back to where he'd picked up the Lap Dancer – but could go to other strip clubs on the East Side of New York.

He was now getting tired from all that driving, and was thinking about just giving up for the night, when he noticed a drunk girl with her boyfriend, sitting on the stoop to this Brownstone on the Eastside. Pulling over to confront them; he rolled down the window and questioned them.

Mercedes: "Excuse me; but, I was looking for this nightclub where the men, you know, have ladies dance before them. I was told there is one similar to this in this area. Could you direct me, if you know of this nightclub?"

Young male: "Yes there is one in this area; but if I tell you, you might get lost. I'm drunk and have no sense of direction, sorry brother man!"

Mercedes: "And what about you sweetheart, do you know of a nightclub?"

Young girl: "Yeah, I can tell you! Go down to the corner and turn left and then right and head down Second

Avenue to Seventh Fifth first and make a right and you'll find it there in the middle of the block."

Mercedes: "What did you say; I can't hear you. Can you come closer to the car please?" Walking over to the car standing in the street; she goes about explaining to him what she did a few seconds ago. He opened the car door and got out and stood next to her. She pointed down the block at the light and told him how to get there. "Oh, I understand now! Make a left at the light....then a right.....!"

Hitting her over the head with a Blackjack; causing her to slump and fall. He grabbed her up and threw her into the front seat. Her boyfriend, who was slow to react was also hit over the head and knocked out cold! He then jumped back into the car; and sped down the street heading straight for the FDR parkway south. He would drive with her stuffed into the front floor, until he reached South Street, where they were constructing a new high-rise behind a barrier. Taking her out of the front seat and behind the barrier, he had sex with her and then strangled her to death. Leaving her body where it would be seen the next morning. He drove away and fled across the Brooklyn Bridge and then down Flatbush to the Belt Parkway East to Howard Beach and home.

He had now stepped out of his normal pattern and would now elevate his seizures to whoever was vulnerable to his attack. To him this had been a more exuberating kill then all the others. Killing a decent somewhat upper class yuppie made him feel as though he could kill anyone he wanted. Arriving back at the house, he'd bathe and make something to eat while watching XXX films on his DVD. Hours would go by before his anxiety would diminish enough for him to sleep. Later his mother would come over from the Main House and find him uncovered and cover him. She would take up his dirty clothes and bring them back to the house to wash and iron them. If only she knew who was really sleeping in that bed, she'd have him snuffed out and buried in the backyard.

Police Headquarters: "What can we do for you mister?"

Boyfriend: "I want to report my girlfriend missing from last night. I live at 334 East Fifty-Sixth Street. My girlfriend and I both had too much to drink and were sitting on our front steps of our building. I don't know what happen, but, I woke up with this bump on my head, and I don't remember how it got there. I went into the apartment and she wasn't there, so I called her cell phone and I heard it ringing outside in front of the building. When I went back downstairs and dialed it again, I found it in the curb underneath a car. Now, she would never leave to go anywhere without her phone, let alone without telling me. I know something has happen to her; so, what can you do put a call out to all patrol cars?"

Police Headquarters: "What's her name and give us a description of what she looks like. Maybe being so drunk she might've just walked off somewhere. We'll take your information and put it into our data system – but, we cannot start a missing person report until twenty-four hours has past. Here; let me take a look at that bump there on your head. You didn't go to the hospital yet did you?"

Boyfriend: "No, I didn't think about that; I was just concern about Mandy my girlfriend, and I came here as quickly as I could. Here, the bump is right here; look!"

Police Headquarters: "That's not a bump; someone hit you with a Blackjack or something like it. What time did you say you were sitting on the front steps and the last time you say her?"

Boyfriend: "I don't remember anything to tell you the truth! And, who would hit me over the head with a Blackjack! Wait; something is coming back to me – wait, I remember her talking with someone from the sidewalk and the person was in a black car – yes, he was asking about a men's club in the area. I can see her talking with him and then, then that's all I can remember. What; do you think someone kidnapped her?"

Police Headquarters: *"I can't say now; but do me a favor and go sit over there until I get my superior to come down. It'll take a few minutes or more; thank you!"*

The dump truck was pulling up to the gate to back into the construction site to unload. When he got out the truck to open the gate, he noticed a body behind the mound of dirt. As he walked over to see if she was alive or dead; he noticed marks around her neck, as though she'd been strangled and her clothes above her head. But what really caught his eyes, were the two hand prints next to her shoulders, like the person had sex with her before killing her.

He ran back to his truck and got on the radio to tell the dispatcher to call the police. He'd forgotten his cell phone and had to use whatever manner of communication to get the police there in a hurry. He would sit in his truck watching the sunrise, waiting for the police. There would be no work done on the site that day. The police had shut down the site for a full investigation. Plaster cast of the hands would be made to match them with the killer, whenever they found him. And a removal of all dirt surrounding the body would be taken in for analyzation back at the CSI lab.

Waleed Yaser

Police Sergeant: *"Hello sir may I ask your name please. I'm Sergeant Tougnut and, I hear you're enquiring about a missing person. Ah; could you give me her name and address to verify whom you're speaking?"*

Boyfriend: *"My name is Walter Knott and my girlfriends name is Mandy Macy; and we both live at 334 East Fifty – Sixth Street, apartment 12 – have you found her. Is she in the hospital or something – tell me; is she alright?"*

Police Sergeant: *"Come with me son; we're going to my office upstairs." The Sergeant and he took the elevator to the second floor. One could hear the howling coming the walls above; he was told about her body being found and that he needed to try and remember more of what happen that night. His hands would be matched to the plaster cast, but it turned out not to be an exact match, thus ruling him out.*

Ring! Ring! Ring! Waking up from his sleep in his reclining chair; he'd fallen asleep late last night, only to be woken up early by the phone call. On the other end, was Mary Lake, who'd gotten a call from the Captain about the discovery of the body on the construction site.

Detective Lopez: *"Okay, I'll meet you down at the morgue. I'll take me about half an hour to get there. Okay bye!" He drove down the FDR parkway with light and serine blaring. Starting the day this early for a victim of the Strangler was not normal – did he make a mistake by*

dropping something of his, or have they found semen —
something he'd never left before on the other victims.

Detective Lake: "Oh; so you're here now — here come take
a look — he moved up the chain on society's ladder. Here; I
want you to meet the Ambassador of Monaco's daughter
Mandy Macy."

Detective Lopez: "The shit has now hit the fan full blast!
Now, we're never going to get a minutes rest, until he's
found."

Detective Lake: "No, nothing has changed for us! The Vice
President has given directives not to block the Secret
Service of Monaco and our Services while they go about
this city looking for this murderer. He's killed the wrong
girl my friend! Now, all we have to monitor is the search
and find of the killers of these Johns. They have the palm
print he left during the rape and murder of this lady."

Detective Lopez: "You mean he left evidence this time that
is traceable down to his hands. Oh, this is really good!
They know he drives a Mercedes with black carpet and
also a hand print! What better group of people to be
tracking down this asshole. They'll have him in handcuffs
really soon now. I bet they have Satellite spying down on
him right now."

Waleed Yaser

Detective Lake: "Okay Hector; listen, we have more than seven hours before we have to be back on the job. We'll put male decoy's back out on the street tonight. We'll focus both on Hell's Kitchen and Chelsea areas – you in Hell's Kitchen and me down in Chelsea with the girls."

Detective Lopez: "So, we split up tonight – you sure you won't need me – you know we always work together but now you want to split up. Okay; let's do it!"

Detective Lake: "I'm doing this because the last girl was a stripper and many of the strip clubs are in Chelsea. If he shows up in Chelsea I'll beep the Secret Services boys to come get his ass. Better they work him over then us! Maybe they'll even extradite him to Monaco."

Leaving the morgue in their separate cars; they both went back to their homes and rested for what was to turn out to be destiny into the unknown!

Later that night; after the mid-shift meeting with Captain Wise; both detectives when their own ways. It was well after sunset that both undercover operations began. All was going well on both perspectives; nothing out of the nature of things happen neither in Chelsea nor in Hell's Kitchen. It was coming up on 1 a.m. when things began to change.

Lopez and his undercover team were looking at this group of men auguring with Lowdown the Pimp. It seemed Lowdown had had enough with these Women coming into his area taking up space and these Johns. His money was being taken from him and he wanted his piece of the cut. Walking over to see what the commotion was, Lowdown had stood there holding his right cheek from the blood dripping onto his six hundred dollar silk shirt. Other men were trying to hold Lowdown back from either getting another slash across the face or the razor holding woman from getting Pimp whipped. It was most likely the former than the latter.

John: "Calm down brother Lowdown – it ain't that bad of a cut – just a few stitches will cover it and give you a pretty birthmark…. Lol lol!"

Lowdown: "That bitch better be gone by the time I get back – otherwise I'll shot her in the ass; and nobody will want to sniff it again. Someone take my keys and get my Cadillac Eldorado parked over there; and take me to the Harlem Hospital." Walking away holding his cut face he got into his car and had himself driven to get stitches.

Detective Lopez: 'Oh; different lady but same pearl handle razor – I'll keep an eye on her tonight and if she picks up a John, I'll follow them. This time Hector; set your car up at the corner and just wait.' It was now coming up on 2:30 a.m. when he noticed the lady taking a ride with a John in his car. Allowing them to get in front of him about half a

Waleed Yaser

block, he got into his car and followed at a safe distance behind them.

Uptown they drove for more than ten minutes before stopping by Morningside Park. They parked the car on 123rd and Morningside Avenue and walked into the park. Parking his car half a block from theirs and walking to the park, he found they had not gone into the park but, had taken a seat near the entrance to the park. Standing behind the tree watching what would transpire, Lopez wanted to radio for assistance, but thought twice about it. What if they were just on a date having sex – he would waste the time of the officers who were undercover for just this. He would handle whatever happens from this moment forward.

He was still standing behind the tree watching, when he noticed the woman standing over him with her face against his face kissing him. When she took her face away; he noticed the pale look in the man's face and stone stare expressed in his eyes. What had this woman done to this man – she either poisons him with drugs or hypnotized him. Lopez continued to watch the woman go behind some bushes and disappear. She reappeared and grabbed the man with one hand and picked him up off the bench and carries him behind the bushes.

Detective Lopez: 'What the hell – she's carrying him with one hand – what strength this woman has for such a petite woman ; no wonder she's not afraid of Pimps like

Lowdown. Where is she taking him – Hector don't go in shooting just investigate and maintain your cool brother man. Okay; let's take a look!' Walking slowly behind the bushes; he loses the two of them from sight. He looks over the other side and sees nothing, and turns back to check if he missed something. Backtracking his steps; he notices a manhole cover slightly with leaves. He bends down and pries open the cover with his badge. Looking down into the dark hole; he listens for footsteps which are not heard. He takes out his little flashlight and shines it into the hole to see what was before him, if he chooses to enter.

Gathering up the nerve to climb down into the dark hole, he takes the first few steps on the ladder and enters. Now on the ground he shines his light down the corridor. What he sees before him is steps leading down to a hallway of water. The water was from the floor to the ceiling of the hallway. For him to even think about swimming through that water, he'd probably need scuba gear at the lease.

Detective Lopez: "No guts, no glory!" Taking out a plastic bag for gathering evidence, he places his gun inside and takes the plunge into the water. 'I hope I can hold my breath for the duration?' Putting the flashlight in his mouth and taking one large breath, he dives in and begins swimming. Seeing nothing in front of him but this very long hallway; he realizes that this one breath wasn't enough to make it. Seeking a air pocket someplace – he sights one place that looked like a doorway and he swam in and up. There above him was a four or five inch space where air existed. Not wanting to exhaust all the air for his return swim, he takes one breath and dives back under. Just when he was about to swim on, he noticed a bright light emitting in the water. Holding his breath he waits and watches what might be coming his way.

The light grew brighter until just before his eyes walked by this very old looking woman in torn clothes. Her skin looked crackly dry and her hair balding with patches of hair on her head. This was truly one very ugly woman; but why was she walking and not swimming. Why wasn't she wearing a breathing device – why was she admitting light! Swimming back up to get another breath of air; he held himself there by bracing himself up.

Detective Lopez: 'This is bullshit! What have I gotten myself into now! How is this woman? Why are they down here…..' He felt a hand around his ankle and he took one breath, before being pulled down into the water. He was being dragged towards the other end of the hallway. Could he hold this one breath for however long; before coming to the end which was how much farther. He had to breath, but couldn't because he'd drown for sure – but he had to breath and now, and now…. Gasping for any air he took into his lungs more than a gallon of water; but, to his amazement he was breathing normally – water in his lungs and he's breathing. 'What the hell; what kind of water is this – I'm alive I won't drown!'

He was then grabbed by two or three hands as he got to the end of the hallway. They carried him up the steps and into a large room which was slightly lit by the glow from the bodies of these very old looking women. All were very ugly with crackly skin and torn clothes. They took him and placed him in one chair facing the women who all stood in a circle.

Detective Lopez: 'Now, I'm really in the shit! I know I can get through the water without drowning; but, I can't move through it as fast as they can. I would surely be caught and brought back to this room.' "Uh; excuse me please. What are you going to do with me?"

No one said anything they just stood there humming and swaying back and forth. Suddenly another woman came into the room with another man in her hands. She dropped the body near the doorway and walked over to Lopez and stared in his face. Though her face was old and crackly; her eyes were young and vibrant. She must've been one very beautiful woman at one time. And then she spoke.

Cathy: "Why is his soul still in his body? Who brought him here living?" She turned her attention to the circle and when no one answered, she took up the body she brought in and stood him up and stuck her tongue into his mouth. A glow emitted from the Johns body and then transferred into hers. She then dropped the body and went into the circle.

Less than what seemed an hour; another woman came into the room with a body of her own. She looked over at Lopez and then at the circle, before taking up her John and doing the same to hers. She too went into the circle and joined in on what seem to be praying. It went on for maybe thirty minutes before breaking up. Stepping forward to confront Lopez was this short pudgy woman. She stood for a second before speaking to him – her words were short and forward.

Ms. Rue: "Why have you come here and who are you? You have discovered us but you will never tell the upside about us!"

Detective Lopez: "I am police officer Hector Lopez of the city of New York. I have found this place because I was tracking the killers of Prostitutes and Johns in this city. It happens that one of your women caught my eye, so I followed her and this is where she led me. She was a very beautiful woman before getting into this hole and now that I'm here, I see all the women are very old. Could you tell me why, all you women are very old and living down here?"

Ms. Rue: "A police man uh? So you work for the Mafia up there? And, we do not kill Prostitutes only Johns. We do this only to be alive again. We were placed here by the Mafia back in 1917 because we would not allow them to enslave us. And so, our souls are trapped here until we get revenge from those who put us here. The Mafia clan of Salami, Pasta and Bolognese – once one of their family members is killed our souls will be released from this gravesite you find us in. But now you have come, and we still have three more girls who need to be revived by taking the souls of these Johns. Our new lives will take us from this grave to the hereafter on a new level of death, maybe even heaven.

Detective Lopez: "So, three more men have to die so you may live. Why kill these men when you have a way out of this. You said there are three Mafia families out there, who can transform your lives to a heaven or wherever. Well, I can help you accomplish this by not killing anymore innocent people."

Ms. Rue: "Tell me how you can do this and it could save your life."

Detective Lopez: "As far as the three families you spoke of – well, two of them live here in the New York area. We've been trying for years to put them behind bars. But we can never gather evidence or informers to take to a

79

Prosecutor. What say I help you get your revenge – but, you must not kill anymore Johns.

Hector explained to Lady Rue what he could offer with his police department access to records, which were able to locate members of each of these families. He offered to escort two of the ladies that Lady Rue would choose to come alone on the venture. And, that he would make a false arrest so to get them into custody. And, once they were in handcuff, he would help the ladies return them back to this room for judgment.

Ms. Rue: "And what's to keep you from running, once we allow you to leave?

Detective Lopez: "I give you my word as a man! Plus, I want to see you women at peace in your next world. It was wrong for them to impose upon you slavery or death. I can only wonder what it was like back in your day."

Ms. Rue: "I was the Renaissance in its hay day! Music, art, entrepreneurship, and many idea's that could be thought up! There was even that little city in Oklahoma called Tulsa; where many from Harlem moved to back in 1915 to become businessmen, and doctors. Many of my first black customers, who could pay, moved out there to make a life for themselves and families. I wished I moved out there before these Mafia people moved in on Harlem."

Detective Lopez: "Oh, you mean Tulsa; well, they burned that city down and murdered hundreds of Black People.

What, you didn't know about that? I'm quite sure; they had some news about it here in Harlem back then. It happens back in 1921; when a black shoeshine boy brushed up against a white elevator operator when the elevator shifted. She screamed out rape or something like that, and all hell broke loose. They say the red necks were going to hang the shoeshine boy but, some black men coming from the first war....."

Ms. Rue: "Yes; many men from Harlem were going to war just before our being kidnapped and placed down here back in 1917. Yes; I think the war started back in 1914 I believe and it took three years before America sent troops over."

Detective Lopez: "Yeah well; as I was saying. These black men who fought in that war, decided not to allow this shoeshine boy to hung, and they went to the jail with their guns and took that boy home. Well, whitey didn't like that so, the War of all wars broke out in Tulsa and lasted over 12 or more hours with three thousand black people killed! It was all because of how the blacks lived not because of that white girl. The blacks were rich and the whites were dirt poor! I'd wished I had been there at that time; I'd had killed as many whitey as they killed us. They even say the Government loan them a plane to bomb them from the air. Now what kind of shit is that if you ask me! Anyway; let's get back to your request. I will take two of your best and most pretties girls with me and we will trap one of these family members to bring here so you and your girls can go free finally."

Ms. Rue: "Okay mister officer; I will trust you to return with my girls and a member of the snakes who put us here. Go with him Staci and Cynthia and watch over him so he doesn't get hurt. We need him; I trust him!"

Detective Lopez: 'I can't wait to see just how beautiful these two women are; because now they look like shit stepped on with twigs!' "Come one girls let's get moving! Oh; mama what do I call you?"

Ms. Rue: "I was called Lady Rue Gaul! I come from Louisiana down by where the Natives and Africans mixed together. My Grandfather was Native and my Grandmother Black Slave! Most of my girls come from my hometown; the others are from New Orleans. Just return my son; and take care of my girls and don't let them get caught. They must be back before daylight comes in; otherwise their souls will burn and be lost forever. Now go and return in a hurry!"

Detective Lopez: "No Lady Gaul; I mean Mama! What I have to do will take all day and most of the night to find these people and watch their moves so we can take them. It is not that easy – I have to get into the computers and put in these names and see what pops up on the screen. I tell you what I will do; I will go back on my own and find out the living places of these people and return in the night to take your two girls with me. I hope you will trust me to return on my own; right Lady Gaul you do trust me don't you?"

Ms. Rue: "Come here my son; bring your ear down here so I may whisper something to you. Listen well son!" She spoke words he didn't know or had ever heard before. "Did you hear what I said son!"

Detective Lopez: "Yes; but I didn't understand a word you were saying Lady Gaul! What did it mean?"

Ms. Rue: "It was a curse if you did not return tomorrow night! The curse will cause sours to grow which will lead to bleeding out all of your blood until death takes over. Now; go and return for my two girls to bring back our salvation. We will pray until you return. Blanch; take him to the other side and return!"

One of the women took Lopez by his hand and took him into the water. The walk was about three minutes long and all the while; he breathed as if he was breathing air. When they got to the other side; he looked at her and was astounded by her beauty. She turned and went back into the water, as the dim light got dimmer until it was gone. Climbing back up the ladder, he got out and headed straight for his car. It didn't dawn on him until he got to his car; that his clothes were dry and not wet from being in *the water. Anyway; he got in and started the car and pulled off. He headed straight for the Precinct. Not only was his job finding these Mafia people going to be hard, but making sure he'd returned that night was also bothering him.*

Mercedes: 'Who can I pay to take my position tonight at the restaurant? I'm getting that itching feeling again, and it needs scratching tonight. Maybe I'll get my cousin Leonardo to take a night off from delivering pizza, and come stand in for me. I'll give him a hundred dollars for the night, and he'll be happy.' Dialing his cell phone he got his cousin while he was still sleeping. "Get your ass up Leo if you want to make a hundred dollars. I need you to stand in for me at the restaurant tonight. All you have to do is look on the reservation book for the peoples name and then escort them to their tables. A easy night and one hundred in your pocket. Okay come by and get the money before I leave tonight. I'll be in the pool house when you come okay!" 'Now that I got that out of the way, let me get my clothes together for tonight. If you're going after high-class you dress high-class. Yes; silk shirt, linen pants and a nice black silk jacket. Damn boy do you look good! Those babes are going to fall all over you tonight, and, when they do – I'll snatch out their souls and spit on it – I am a true lover for sure.'

Detective Lopez: 'Okay; let's try Salami family first!
Looking, looking, looking – no, everybody is either too old
or female. Okay, now the Pasta family – here, one thirty
year old but, no, in jail for ten years. Okay, let's look here;
male 38 years old but, still, in a mental hospital – most
likely acting crazy to stay out of jail – okay another pasta
family member a male and still no good; has AIDS
confined to bed waiting for death any minute. Okay; let's
try the Bolognese family; okay, here one, two, three all
females and yes; one male 29 years old, goes by the name
Vincent. Okay, let me get the particulars on him. He lives
with the family in the compound on Howard Beach
Queens. Went to Princeton for five years – must've
partied the first four – has degree in finances and drives a
Black Mercedes. He'll do just, just....wait a minute! He
drives a Black Mercedes Benz AMG 500 2009......no way!
This shit is starting to smell like – if he's the guy we've
been looking for all this time – no, it can't be that easy!
Though, it really has been very hard trying to catch him in
action – the carpet fibers; I bet they could belong to an
AMG class.' "Detective Mulligan I want you to call CSI and
ask them if those fibers found on the dead girl at Central
Park, matches the AMG class type cars. Have him call me
directly when you get him." 'If this is our guy; then we got
his ass! But, I can't tell anyone – he has to go to Lady Gaul
in exchange for not killing anymore Johns – hell; isn't no
skin off my back. He'll do! Now, how do I get close to him

– and what If he is the Strangler; then, he'll like what I'll have in store for him tonight. If he is then he'll go to her like a bee to honey. I know just how I'm going to pull this off. We rid this city of a Serial Killer and the ladies go on to the other side! Okay; his address is!'

Detective Mulligan: "Uh Lopez! The CSI said they can't talk to now but, yeah, it could be from that class of car. A very high end style carpet might've come from that vehicle – is there anything else you want?"

Detective Lopez: "Yeah; when you see Detective Lake this evening tell her I'm chasing down a lead and will call her if it pans out." Leaving the stationhouse and getting into his car, he drove across the Sixty-First Street Bridge into Queens and down Queens Boulevard to the Van Wyck Expressway and then onto Belt Parkway West towards Howard Beach.

It was the middle of the afternoon, as he staked out the family compound. He wasn't sitting long before the gates opened and out drove a Black Mercedes AMG 500. Following at a safe distance, he continued up Rockaway Boulevard pulling into a parking lot, where he got out and walked into the Supermarket. Seizing the opportunity to search his car, he pulls his car up to the bumper and gets out walking to the passenger side of the car. Using a electronic device to gain access via the secret code, he opens the door and gathers a small sample of the carpet. He knew that this would be thrown out by the court as evidence, so taking it to be analyzing for a match was really his purpose. Before getting back in his car, he placed a homing device under the bumper, so, when he sought to find him again later that evening it wouldn't be a timely matter. Driving out of the parking lot, he drove to downtown Manhattan to the lab of the CSI.

There he would offer this sample – not telling them it was from the car of a Mafia son – to verify for himself whom his target for tonight was. He sat in the hallway waiting for almost two hours, when the CSI agent came to him with the results.

CSI: "Detective Lopez; where did you get this sample of carpet? It's an exact match to that found on the hooker. You will be able to make an arrest – now, let me contact my superiors about your findings. You can sit here until I return or you can go call your superiors and ask for a taskforce to roll with you. I'll be back in five minutes okay!"

Detective Lopez: 'No, I'm not waiting for you to return; I'm leaving as soon as you're out of sight.' "Okay I'll be sitting here waiting for you!" 'Okay Hector; he's gone now, you be gone too. Get to your car and make haste in homing in on that car. I'll follow him until night comes, and then make my way over to pick up the girls.' Homing in on the Mercedes signal, he was taken back to the compound on Howard Beach. The suspect was back in his hole, most likely just waiting for the night to come, before prowling the streets for his next prey. It was coming up on 6 p.m. as he sat in his car watching waiting for him to come out again. But when the time got near 7 p.m. he decided to just go and get himself ready tonight. Driving back to his place in the Bronx; he was not surprised to be confronted by his partner, Detective Lake.

Detective Lake: "What's going on with you Hector? Why you'd disappear from the lab, when he asked you to convey your findings with Chief Notting and Captain Wise? What are you hiding from us – they say you found carpet fibers that a exact match to those found on the striper, and here you want to keep it from us – explain yourself Hector. Tell us what is really going on with you. You don't show up in the morning for debriefing of the night's occurrences and then you show up at CSI with a carpet sample. Where did you get this sample Hector; whose car does it belong to and why haven't you proceeded with an arrest of this suspect?"

Detective Lopez: "I have nothing to say right now Mary! When I get more substantial evidence on this car and the suspect, I will forward it on to the appropriate authorities. But, right now I'm just chasing a hunch of mines. I'd ask you to come alone but you can't right now. Listen; I have to go get dressed for tonight's roll call, where I'll answer any question the Captain wants to hear. I'll see you tonight; okay bye!" Walking by Detective Lake into his building he went inside and hurried to look out the window five flights down on the street. There he saw Detective Lake and two other detectives in an unmarked car, talking about what he knew, was their staking out of him. He would outsmart them by going down to the garage and taking out his baby for a drive around town tonight. Parked and under a cover; was his 1979 black Monte Carlo. He would use this to surely blend in as he hopes to stakeout the compound after picking up the girls.

He hurried across town into Harlem to park near Morningside Park. It was nearing 8 p.m. when he climbed down the hole and swam to the room. Upon coming up on the other side, he was greeted by Lady Gaul herself smiling as he walked in.

Detective Lopez: "Tonight ladies will be the last night you will have to stay in this appalling place. I wish you all a safe travel to the next world; but, first we have to capture this man I have chosen from the family of Bolognese! He is very young and handsome. My plan is to follow his car around until I see a opportunity to send one of your girls out to entice him. He will ask that she get into his car, which she will. Most likely he will try and get physical with her – you will have those pretty pearl handle razors with you right." Each of the women reached under their torn dresses and pulled out a razor. "Good; now, once he tries to strangle you, you will take out the razors and place it against his neck. Once you have him subdued I will come in and place handcuff on him. I will then place him in the back seat of his car – you two will then hold him and keep him from screaming…..”

Ms. Rue: “They will put him to sleep only, and you will be able to bring him back here with no difficulties.”

Detective Lopez: “Okay mama, and once we have him in the car; I will leave my car there and pick it up later. I have a police sticker to put into the dashboard to make sure they don’t tow my car. Oh; I forget you don’t know anything about what I am saying. Anyway; mama we will leave from here in about one hour.” Sitting there watching his watch; his anxiety level grew and grew, waiting for that time to go out and catch the Strangler before he kills someone else. He wanted his desires to be vented against these ladies, who were well able to fend him off. “Okay ladies; I cannot sit here waiting anymore. Let’s go get this man! Who’s coming with me Lady Gaul I forget?”

Ms. Rue: “Staci and Cynthia are going with you. Okay girls go bring back this man so we can finally go home!”

Already at the door, Hector was stepping down into the water, when both ladies took him by the arms and walked him through the water. The light emitting from the two of them made Hector warm within. He was helping both worlds to rid itself of a Serial Killer. When they arrived at the other end; their beauty was evident. Both were light brown skin with shiny black hair and the most seductive eyes ever.

As they drove down the FDR towards the bridge; Hector turned on the homing device listening for the signal to start beeping at a rapped pace. He would first drive to the suspect house, and if not there he would cross the bridge back into Manhattan and continue his search.

When they neared the compound; no signal was heard, so he turned around and headed down the Belt Parkway to drive through Brooklyn and then into Manhattan. The drive took them almost an hour – an hour that could've cost someone their life – when the signal began to beep at a steadier rate. He was getting closer to his victim. He crossed the Brooklyn Bridge and determines that the signal took him to Tribeca. He pulled the car up near Hudson Street and Chambers Street. The signal was now very high as if the car was parked next to his. When he noticed this well dressed Italian man coming out a restaurant, he knew that that might be his man. Asking the ladies to sit inside and wait, he got out and ran across the street to see which car this man would get into. When he crossed the street, he saw him enter a Black Mercedes. Running back over to his car, he put it in gear and headed around the corner to catch up with the car. Having his *homing device still on, the beeping was steady. Turning off the homing device because it was becoming annoying to his ear, he looked into his rear view mirror at the two ladies. Oh, if they were only real living ladies, he'd have a ball for sure. Very classy refined ladies, who know how to entice a man's pants off and his empting of his wallet, getting what they want.*

He continued to follow the Mercedes uptown to Park Avenue and Fortieth Street. The Mercedes slowed down as he trolled looking for women of his liking. Ceasing the opportunity; Hector drove ahead of him and told Traci to get out and walk slowly up the street. Driving ahead of him and double parking with his lights flashing; he looked in his mirror and watched for the Mercedes.

As predicted; he drove up to Traci and stopped in the street. Still watching in his mirror, Hector took out his handcuffs and placed them on the front passenger chair. He looked back in the mirror to see Traci come into the street, walk in front of the car and got into the passenger door. The trap had been sprung; and the mouse was soon to be caught.

He watched the Mercedes cut all the way to the other side of the street, and head down one of the side streets. Turning his homing device back on, Hector cut across the street and drove down a side street hoping to intersect the Mercedes as it came up or down the street. Speeding to the corner of Lexington Avenue, he looked for the

Mercedes. Not seeing it he continued to the next cross street; which was Third Avenue. Stopping at the corner he noticed the Mercedes heading uptown on Third Avenue. Waiting for him to get a few seconds on him, he turned on red and followed him up Third Avenue. They drove for more than ten minutes with the lights and traffic, only to turn right onto Ninety-Sixth Street, heading towards the FDR Drive Parkway. Catching up to the car, Hector watched to see if he would head back downtown to the construction site where he'd dropped off his last body. But, he headed North instead. Closely following behind him and trying not to be mixed up too much in the traffic, the Mercedes took Harlem River Drive North. Still behind the car without being noticed; Hector kept the car in sight. When the Mercedes got off the parkway at 143rd Street; Hector was close behind him. The Mercedes turn right and parked in a very dark spot next to the parkway. His lights went off and he most likely was about to commit another attempt at killing.

Parking the car just up the street but far enough away not to spook the Strangler; Hector got out and slowly walked towards the car. He didn't see any movement from what little light there was, so he continued walking up towards the car. When he got to the back of the Mercedes, he noticed the head of the man – he was not moving but still – had he gotten there in enough time to stop her from cutting his throat. Looking now into the driver's side window, he could see that she had everything under control. The guy had both his hands propping himself up so not to be cut by the sharp blade. Opening the door Hector said on three words. "You're under arrest!" Taking the suspect by his collar and pulling him out of the car, he threw him up against the car and told him to spread eagle. Doing so, Hector handcuffed him and told him to get into the back seat of the car. Running back to his car, he got Cynthia and the two of them got into the Mercedes and drove off.

Detective Lopez: "Well, well, well! I guess you never thought you'd ever get caught this soon did you? You're going to face a trail like you've never thought. Now, are you not the son of deceased G'dfather Vito III Bolognese? You may answer!"

Vincent Bolognese: "Yes I am the son; and my family has too many connections in many courts, so I will most likely spend ten years in a mental hospital and then get out to do it all over again. I will say no more until I speak with my Lawyer officer what's your name. You'll be walking the beat at Forty-Second Street after my lawyer gets finish with you!"

Detective Lopez: "Well sonny; you won't be seeing any lawyer or a court house. You're going to be judged by a different court and I don't ever want to be in your shoes. Shut his mouth up ladies!"

Cynthia leaned over and kissed him; thus putting him in a state of transience. Hector drove over to Morningside Park and parked the Mercedes – where it would later be found with no traces of the driver. Taking his body out and walking him over to the manhole, they lowered his body inside and all three disappeared within.

Captain Wise: "It's been four hours and counting detective Lake; and Lopez's has yet to call, radio or come by to ask me how I'm doing! Where is this partner of yours? Has the man gone dumb crazy knowing we've got this whole city wound tight as we look for this Strangler and John Killer. Oh; he'll be on report the minute I see his ass! Tell me what he told you the last time you saw him?"

Detective Lake: "Well sir; he just said he had a lead to look into and that he'd be here before the shift began. I have tried calling his cell, but it goes straight to his answering service. I have no idea where this man might be. We'll just have to wait him out and see what happens next. Can I go back on the streets Captain; we have a city to monitor!"

Walking out of the Stationhouse; Lake got into her car and sat for a few moments thinking. 'Brother; I hope you know what you're doing!' Turning the key and driving off into the night life of New York City and whatever was awaiting her.

Waleed Yaser

Detective Lopez: "Hey bone head wake up! Wake your ass up boy; you've got Judgment Day before your eyes. Wake up and face your punishment!" SLAP! SLAP!

Vincent Bolognese: "Where am I? Who are you and what am I doing here. What is this place, a interrogation room? Well, I'm not speaking until my lawyer gets here!"
Looking around the room, Vinnie knew this was no interrogation room; he'd seen many before but none like this. Over in the corner he could slightly see the figures of women standing with their backs turned to him. "Who are those women over there – what do they want from me?"

Detective Lopez: "Well Vincent; let me introduce you to some of your past family members handy work. These women here were put in this hall by your Great grandfather Vito Bolognese, your Uncle Joseph Pasta and Lucky Salami. It all took place way back in 1917 in Harlem and it seems very poetic that now you're here in Harlem facing the same predicament as they did way back when. Let me introduce you to the ladies of the evening." One by one they turned to face him – their faces old and cracking skin they each gave their names and stood to the side.
The last to stand in front of him was Lady Gaul. "And last but not least is Ms. Rue. She will speak to you now, so pay close attention, because your soul rest upon it!"

Ms. Rue: "In 1917 I had a brothel not too far from here. I was a respectable owner of the house and my ladies were gems in the rough. And, then along came your family members; who tried to force me into working for them. I declined to do so and they tied us up here and told us we would die slowly. Well, I prayed upon our souls that we stay here until we got revenge from the members of this Mafia family. Now is that day! We have you a great grandson to one of those men, and now your soul will remain here alone until the day all dead are raised. We will ascend to wherever G'd want us! And I must say, we are so much in a hurry to leave from here. So, we will all one after one kiss you goodbye – oh I forgot to put the curse upon you - MIsfy secbula walayyah nottocillar colltetnur fihialli! And may your soul rest in agony!"

One by one the ladies walked up and removed a bit of his soul with a simple kiss! The last was Ms. Rue as her beauty returned to her and her eyes lit up with joy!

Detective Lopez: "Ms. Rue; nobody will ever believe me concerning this story so, I will never tell of it as long as I live. But, I am very happy to have helped all of you ladies reach your hereafter! May G'd have mercy upon your souls forever!" Looking over at Vincent as he slowly drifted into a state of limbo. Hector looked into his eyes and saw the pain that was becoming upon his being.

Waleed Yaser

"There is no pity for murderers like you boy rest in Hell! Okay ladies; how do we leave from here me first?"

Ms. Rue: "Yes sonny you go first. You may walk as the water has subsided until our souls ascend and then it will return to enclose this place forever. Go and may G'd send you a love to keep you happy Amen!"

Making his way down the hallway; Hector's thoughts were racing about who could come into his life and bring him the happiness he's been searching for all his life. But, those were just word from a Witch right. Climbing the ladder to the top he got onto the ground and moved the manhole cover so their souls wouldn't have any obstructions.

He stood there for more than five minutes when all of a sudden; a light flashed before him and a gust of wind almost knocked him over, and the manhole cover returned to it place. The ladies had now gone to the other life after this one. Walking down the street past the Mercedes; he put his hand in his pocket for that long walk back to his car. He noticed something in his pockets and pulled it out. Behold before his eyes was one of the Pearl Handle Razor's the ladies carried for protection. A gift for helping them or for proving they did exist; either way he was thankful.

Lady Passerby: "Excuse me sir; but can I get the number three subway train in this area?"

Standing before him was one really beautiful woman! She looked half black and Indian or something; but, damn did she look good!

Detective Lopez: "No Miss you cannot catch the three from here. Are you heading uptown or downtown?"

Lady Passerby: "I'm going downtown to see the lights of Time Square. I'm not from here. I'm from Louisiana in a area where the Natives and African's mixed during slavery time. I just took a few weeks vacation to come here to see New York for the first time. Why do you ask where I'm going; I just asked if the train ran in this area?"

Detective Lopez: "I didn't mean to intrude upon you; but, I could give you a ride if you'd accept. My car is not too far from here and as we walk we can get to know each other better."

Lady: "And why would I like to get to know more about you! Plus, I would never get into a car with a stranger. What is your name sir?"

Detective Lopez: "Oh; excuse me for not introducing myself. I am Detective Hector Lopez of the city of New York. Here's my badge and credentials to prove it." Showing her his Gold Shield he could see she was more receptive. "I'm off for the rest of the evening and would be happy to show you around New York. Maybe we can even have a little dinner if you like?"

Lady: "Well; I think very kindly of you to spend your night with me sir; by the way. Are you married?"

Detective Lopez: "No I am not; not yet that is!"

As the two of them continued to walk down the street; their figures getting smaller and smaller, there was a new life starting and a old one ending. But love and happiness shall forever shine over darkness of despair!

A Prayer for a Dead Soul

Forty-one acres and no mule!

Written By: Waleed Naeem Yaser   November 29, 2011©

Looking down from a high upon a field yet to be plowed, a lonely driver within the tractor, plows up dust which almost blocks out the Sun. Descending down to view a sweat drenched driver, who wipes his forehead, Marvin West takes a moment from the remaining thirty-three acres yet to be done.

Marvin is co-owner of this vast farmland; which was given to him by his Great-grandfather Isium, who was a 'Freed Slave' who made his former Master very rich. After reconstruction and the promised given to the many former slaves, which was the gift of 'Forty Acres and a Mule' – though, the Government never kept their promise (like the forgotten promised to the Indigenous People) this former Master West did, by giving a third to the descendents of Isium.

The other owner was Jason West who retained two-thirds for him and his Grandfather – the Great grandson of Master West – who hated how he cared for the land. If not for Marvin, who cared for the land every year, making sure it was plowed over for the coming planting season, Grand pops would've used every resort to take back the land from his son and put it into Marvin's hand to care for. Reaching into his pocket for his cell phone; Marvin made a call to his wife.

Marvin: "I SHOULD BE FINISHED IN ABOUT THREE HOURS HONEY! HAVE DINNER AND A COLD SIX-PACK READY FOR ME, ALRIGHT!"

Pauline: "Why are you yelling fool? I can hear you just well – then you'll be working past Sunset then, okay, the food will be on the stove – I'm going into town for a wash and set! Talk to you when I see you!"

Marvin: "LOVE YOU BABY GIRL, BYE!" Hating himself even more for marrying that high price hussy, he wondered what she really was going into town for. But, focusing his attention back on the task at hand, placing the tractor back into gear, he continued towards the far end of the North side of the farm. It would be well past ten at night before he'd see dinner.

Pulling back to the vantage point of a bird's eye view, we travel across the field as the tractor grows smaller and smaller. We fly over the inner city and head towards the far end of town, where many cars line the dirt paved driveway. Inside the livestock barn, we see cows and pigs being brought and sold as the Auctioneer voice echoed about. We travel upstairs to the back room, where something sinister is about to happen.

Chemist Wilson: "The only words from your mouth that I want to hear Jason, is I have your money in full! Now, how much do you have and if it's not what we agreed upon, I'll take back my product. Hand it over!"

Jason: "Shit stain Wilson – now, don't you trust me? We been doing business for too many years now, and this is how you speak to me. Hell bent boy; if you weren't so good at what you do, I'd tell you to kiss off and take your shit – but, here's your money and have my shit put into my pick-up!"

The Chemist was into all kinds of 'Frankenstein' type shit. You wanted to bring your cows to market faster than your competitor, then, you make a deal with the Chemist and he gives you a fix. Handing the suitcase over to the Chemist – Jason watched to see if he'd count it or run out before someone else could see him and know he and Jason were up to no good!

Waleed Yaser

Jason: "Are we good Wilson or not?"

Just peeking into the suitcase and seeing the load of green, Wilson just waved and walked down the back stairs to his car. As we look out the window down at Wilson, he ordered a group of Mexicans to remove the twenty one- hundred pound bags from his wagon, who then placed them into Jason's pick-up truck.

Jason: 'This shit better work like he says it will – I've got all my yearly cash put into making this harvest the best ever! And, that damn Marvin better be finished plowing that back portion – I'm going to test this shit there first, well out of Grandpa's view – he's an Organic man!'

Driving back towards the middle of town, Jason stops off at the local watering hole. Entering through the doors, he notices how empty the place was. All the men of the town were most likely at the auction bidding on livestock. Finding a place at the end of the bar to sit, two drinks were placed before him – one for himself and his guest who'd yet to come.

Bartender: "Jason; you still haven't paid this month rent for use of the bungalow. I know you're good for the cash, but, I have bills also that need paying, so, when do I get the money?"

Jason: "I'll pay you next week okay – that good with you – well, is she back there or not?"

Bartender: "No, haven't seen her yet today."

Jason: "When she comes, give her a bottle of Jack Daniel's to bring with her." Taking up the two drinks and walking out the back door, he walked to one of the eight bungalows and entered. Inside he sat down on the reclining chair and leaned back. Grabbing the remote for the big screen, he sat watching an old movie with Eva Garner as he sipped his drink.

It was getting well close to sunset when the door opened and in walked the woman. She had in her hands two brown paper bags filled with groceries. Placing them on the counter she walks over and takes the glass out of Jason's hand, who had fallen asleep while watching the TV.

Jason: "Oh; I see you finally made it in one piece. You're cooking dinner aren't you, because, I'm hungry as hell. What's in the bag – and, did the bartender give you that bottle of JD to bring with you? Here, let me help you unpack while you start cooking. Nice hairdo sweetheart – here, let me feel it!"

Pauline: No, your hands are dirty! I can't stay long tonight – that husband of mines is driving me crazy. He's smothering me so I can't become the woman I am. I need attention, I need comfort and most of all I need good sex. He's always tired and can't hold up his stamina in the bed….."

Jason: "I guess that's why you're here with me right. I give you good sex – so, let's eat, drink and then you can go home to Marvin. He better have that north end finished when I get there tomorrow morning. He was still working the fields when you left this afternoon right?"

Pauline: "He said he'd finish by sunset but, who knows! Let me get cooking – I got some beef ribs and salad fixings for dinner and a cheese cake and ice cream for dessert. Afterwards, we'll have a quickie in the bed and I'll go home to my husband, who'll want a massage before sleeping. I'm planning something and I hope you'll be a part of it. I've put away a considerable amount of cash, and I'm looking on the internet some property in Florida to purchase. I've had enough of Marvin – it's time for me to leave and make whatever future I can for myself, before I get any older."

Jason: "You shouldn't have married that nigger in the first place – don't get me wrong, I know you're half nigger, and that doesn't stop me from loving you – anyway, enough of talk like this; it's depressing shit to listen to. If you're going to leave then just leave. Me, I have my land here and I won't just pack up and leave all that to Marvin – well, maybe he could be my share cropper while I'm not here – nah, I don't think so Pauline. I'll come visit you every now and then, but to leave my land; no, I won't not for any pussy!"

Pauline: "Yeah well, I bet you also got some nigger blood deep inside you – I know your Great great-grandmother was creeping at night just like her husband did with those slaves! So, watch your mouth! Now, let's eat!"

Marvin: *"Hey Pop's; how's them old bones today – you having problems with your legs still. Listen, did you see Pauline go out and if so, what time did she leave?"*

Papa West: *"These old bones holding on for an eighty-five year old wouldn't you say? Nah! I've been sitting out here on the porch all day long with my scatter gun by my side – been trying to catch me a rabbit or two for dinner – but, haven't seen anything but field mouse all day long. Your wife must've gone out the back door and out the east end of the barn – didn't see her drive off or anything. You got a minute or two sonny – come sit next to me alright!"*

Marvin: *"Sure do Papa, what's on your mind tonight."* Sitting on the lower stoop next to his legs (like when he was three years old listening to stories about the first world war) he looked up at him wondering what he'd say this time. Been going off lately about how things have changed and things won't get any better before time runs out. *"You want me go get you some moonshine from Mae's place down the road?"*

Papa West: *"No, just want you to listen to what I got to tell you. It might come as a shock but, you need to know anyway. It's about my grand-son and your wife – I think they is having something between them, and if you knew about it you'd shot the two of them. I have no real hard evidence but, I have that feeling that we old people got when something is not right. He's out most of the day while you do all the work, and she's in and out of the farm too going who knows where. They must have some meeting place in town for sure. Anyways just watch yourself for now! Now go fetch me a drink sonny."*

Rubbing the leg of Papa West, Marvin walked into the house and straight to the kitchen. Looking over at the stove, he saw three pots covered with plates. Underneath the plates was his dinner. "Uh, beef stew just like I like it. And, under this plate, is, red beans and rice – that'll go good with the stew – and, here we have the muster greens with smoke turkey wings. My baby can cook." 'I have to start spending more time with her – she is spending too much time in town, and hanging out with them girls at the Salon – she has to understand it's all for our future together. After a few more years of saving up enough money from these harvest; I'm going to sale my share of the farm to Jason, and then go out and purchase my own farm in another state. California is the best place – there I can raise two crops a year – and maybe Pauline and I can start that family she's always talking about. Yes, I'll do that for sure – just two or three more good years and I'm out.' "Hey Papa West you want to eat something before having that drink. Pauline made some real good greens here; your favorite too!"

Papa West made his way into the kitchen and the two of them sat and ate up all three pots of food. For a eighty-five year old man, he had an appetite of a much younger man.

The time was coming up on twelve mid-night when Pauline walked into the back door. Seeing the kitchen table with emptied pots and the sink filled with plates, said the dinner went over well. Walking towards the back of the house and up the back stairs to one of the master rooms, there laid Marvin in his under wears uncovered with the air conditioner blowing on him, she covered him and got undressed to get into bed. It was then that Marvin woke up and turned over to look at her.

Marvin: "What time is it baby?"

Pauline: "It's about twelve in the morning honey; you okay?"

Marvin: "Nah; was thinking about what Papa said as I laid here trying to sleep."

Pauline: "What the old man say now! Don't let him get you all flustered out – you've got too much work on your hands to be having to listen to his antic – what he's talking now, he wants to plant fruit trees again. Didn't he learn that lesson way back in the seventies, when he lost everything to drought? No, don't do what he tells you Marvin, this is just as much yours as it is his and that no good grandson of his. Listen; I don't want to talk any more about that old man; I want to go to bed. And, adjust the air-conditioner – it's a bit too cold!"

Marvin: "He didn't say anything like that honey; it's just, that he has suspicions about what's going on around here, and, I told him not to worry, that we all will get what is coming to us, whether it's good or bad. Anyway; let's get some sleep. I have to start on the south end of the field tomorrow and then try and get some of the lower part. I want to expand that lower part and maybe put some goats and sheep for the milk. I want to try and make cheese to sell in the Organic Market in town. I have a idea on how to make the cheese but, I will ask one of the Amish farmers to come give me some lessons. I have many plans for this farm – so, I might as well use it before I lose it right?"

Pauline: "Enough thinking now honey; just come to bed! We can talk about that in the morning over breakfast alright?"

Marvin: "Okay baby okay! We'll talk about it then – now, get some sleep – awe; do you want something before going to sleep baby?"

Pauline: "Not tonight Marvin – in the morning okay – I'm tired!"

KNOCK! KNOCK! KNOCK!

Bartender: "Jason! Jason, are you up? Its 10 a.m. and, I got to get these women cleaning up the bungalows. Jason!"

Jason: "Yeah, yeah I hear you! I'll be out in less than an hour, now give me a break!" 'Get off your ass man; you've got a lot to do today on that north end. You have seeds to go down and the irrigation to set up before employing the fertilizer on the land. I don't know how much of farm is ready for planting but at least I can have the north end finished. If this fertilizer works as Wilson says then, I should be able to get two harvests this year and double my money. I can plant corn and get the

Ethanol companies to purchase the first harvest and, then supply the supermarkets with the second harvests. Hell, the people are already eating shit corn with all the GMO going on in this market, my corn shouldn't matter one bit. Let me get dressed and leave; been here too long already!'

Driving down the main street of town, Jason grabs up six Mexican workers off the street. He would use them the next week or so, letting them sleep and eat in the barn. Pulling out his cell phone to make a call, Jason pulls over to the curb in front of the Convenient Store. Handing one of the Mexican's a fifty dollar bill, to purchase whatever they wanted, he made his call.

Jason: "Yo Marvin it's me Jason! Just want to know if that north end is ready for planting? It is! Good; I'll be there in less than twenty minutes. I picked up six Mexicans to do the north side – I want you to tell Pauline that, she'll have to cook for six extra people the next few weeks. Is there anything you want me to bring you from town? Nothing! Okay, see you when I see you; bye!   HURRY UP YOU MEXICAN! It doesn't take all day to get a few items – now, which one of you speaks good English – don't need any mistakes when doing the planting, so, who wants to be the spokesman of the group?"

Jamie: "I speak good English mister – everyone else can only say a few words in English. I will explain to them what you want us to do and, make sure the work is complete. Now, how much will we be paid for this work can I ask?"

Jason: "I need this group of men for two weeks or more – and, I can pay four hundred fifty per week - I will use the other fifty for your food which is three meals hot each day. You want beer or other drinks you will have to buy them. I've already given you all fifty dollars which is for you to spend as you will; but, when we get to the farm, you will start working immediately – we have less than seven hours before sunset. Now, where's the other men – why haven't they got back into the pickup!"

Jamie: "They inside getting enough beers to last a few days – there is a place to keep them cold until we finish working the field – like a refrigerator or something in the barn?"

Jason: "The barn is not just a place for storing material – we also have a section for workers, which has a frig, big screen TV and microwave. There is no cooking in the barn; my partner's wife will cook all your meals. Now, let's go, get in the truck!"

Marvin: 'Why did Jason only get six men to work the farm? We need more like twenty to make sure all the planting is completed and the irrigation is set up correctly. Maybe I'll have to go to town and pick up a bunch more laborers. I have to have the south and west end finished by the end of the day, I can save the east end for tomorrow. Oh, let me call Pauline and tell her to hire a cook to help her in the kitchen.' "Hey *baby! Listen, Jason is bringing some workers to the farm today, and he wants you to start cooking for them. I don't want you to work hard, so, call into town and ask some of your friends to get two girls to come here and cook. It's okay with me if we eat Mexican food – if we want something else we can go to town for a night out together. Okay, I'll see you when I get finish this evening." Driving the tractor off as the rows for seeding are etched into the ground, Marvin turns up his music in his headphones as the acres go by and by.*

Arriving at the barn, Jason orders the Mexican workers to unload the pickup and pack every bag in the back of the barn. He would then pull out the small tractor which has the seeding cultivator and load it with seeds. He then takes it to the north end and begins going over the newly turned over soil. It would take Jason four hours to complete this task, as the laborers come behind him with rakes to make sure the rows are covered. The sun was about to set when Jason and Marvin both drove their tractors into the barn for the night.

Marvin: "Jason, did you finish sowing the north field with the wheat seeds?"

Jason: "No Marvin; I'm using that field for raising corn this time around. We can use the east end for the wheat, and south and west ends for whatever you want. I'm using some special seeds this time and I'm hoping to see a big yield when we harvest. That end gets most of the sun for most of the daytime, and it's on a down slope, where the rain water will filter down to."

Marvin: "What kind of seed are they? They're not GMO are they? You know what that will do for future planting don't you. We always use our seeds for corn – been using this seed for over one hundred years. Don't make our life difficult with that stuff."

Jason: "No, I know what I'm doing Marvin. It is not GMO type seed – it's just a different form of organic seed. I got them off the internet from a European farmer in Ireland. Nothing to worry about; let us see what kind of harvest we'll get first, before criticizing my decision."

Marvin: "I trust your decision making – it's just, that we've never used that area for corn – but, go ahead and do what you want. As for the other areas, when will they be seeded?"

Jason: "Listen, I've got these six men working in this area specifically to make sure that this corn grows without disruption. I'll be fertilizing this end in two days. I'm using the water tank tractor; so, if you need it use it before Friday okay?"

Papa West: "Hey girl! Hey; you got anything for me to eat? Come on out here and speak to me girl." Papa West was sitting in his chair on the porch with his shotgun by his side, as Pauline came through the screen door.

Pauline: "What do you want to eat old man? I've got some meatball sandwiches if you want that, or, I can make you a turkey sandwich – which one do you perfer?"

Papa West: "Whatever you got ready for me to eat. Listen girl; you need to leave my badass grandson alone. You got a good man in Marvin – if he could be my grandson, I'd be happy. Jason doesn't care anything about anything but money. He barely takes care of this land – too much work he says – but, Marvin cares for it like it's his..."

Pauline: "It is his land old man; he been working it for years and still he's treated like he's share cropping for you and your family. As for Jason; maybe you should keep your mouth shut and stop feeding my husband's head with all that junk. Now, do you want to eat or not?"

Papa West: "You have one of them Mexican girls bring me out a meatball sandwich and a cold beer or two. As for the other thing; heed my words and stop fooling around against your husband. You'll lose in the end!"

Walking back into the house; she allowed the screen door to slam shut behind her. Walking towards the kitchen she noticed out the window Jason walking into the barn. She ordered one of the girls to make a sandwich and bring it to the old man sitting on the porch. Walking out the back door to the kitchen, she made her way across the driveway into the barn.

Waleed Yaser

Pauline: "Jason; are you alone! Where are you?"

Jason: "I'm here; what are you doing, you want Marvin to catch us together alone. You know we're only to meet in town at the bungalow, and never here on the farm. What is it that you want?"

Pauline: "Your grandfather is putting his nose into my business. He's asked me to stop seeing you – he knows we're lovers, and I'm afraid he'll tell Marvin about us. Marvin told me something a few days ago, about how he was thinking about something but, he wouldn't tell me what it was – I'm sure he must've spoke to your grandfather about us – so, what do we do?"

Jason: Nothing at all! We do nothing but what we've been doing these past few years – and, that's to meet in town and never here on the farm – now, go back inside before someone sees you. I'll take care of the old man – I should've put his ass in the old home a long time ago – maybe I can get the doctor to write something up on him, forcing him to go into storage for awhile. I'll see you later tonight after I finish doing what I have to do. I got the north end to fertilize and then I'm heading into town for next two days. I'll see you not tomorrow but the next day, once things have cooled down a bit."

Walking back towards the house, Pauline entered the back door to the kitchen, and was seen helping the two Mexican girls prepare food. Jason went towards the back of the barn and began reading the instruction on the fertilizer bag. 'For every hundred gallons of water, add twenty pounds of fertilizer, allow one hour before applying to plants. 'Caution' do-not exceed the recommended pounds per hundred gallons'... this tank holds three hundred gallons of water, and I'm to use only sixty pounds – okay, let's see how good this stuff really is – sixty pounds it is and mix well.' Jason didn't want to wait the normal thirty days, before fertilizing, because he wanted to reap the riches from all the money he'd put out for this scientific type fertilizer.

Driving the water tank out of the barn, Jason made his way to the north end, and began spraying the fertilizer on the ground. It took him over two hours to complete the job and he made his way back to the barn, where he would park the tank and then shower in the workers area. He would then head to town and drink till the night was over and the sun begun to rise.

Back at the farm, Papa continued to sit in his chair on the porch, watching and waiting for a rat to scurry within his sight. Inside, both Pauline and Marvin sat in front of the TV watching the movie 'Sparkle' staring Lonette McKee and Irene Clara. They were sitting closer than they had for some time, and Pauline was somewhat touched by the movie, as a single tear fell from her eye.

Marvin: "Very nice movie baby, wouldn't you say?" Looking into her eyes, he tilted his head and kissed her. "Whenever this movie is played – and it's been a very long time since we've watched it together – that, I have forgotten just how much our love mimics the ending. It was something like this that we first met, do you remember baby doll?"

Pauline: She couldn't look him in the face, but held her eyes downward, as the memories forced themselves forward to the present. Her heart quickens and her forehead became moist, as she could only voice just a few words. "How could I not!" Shame raced within her for all she had done to him these past few years – she knew he had worked very hard to give her whatever she wanted – but, her secular values betrayed her with a falsity of what was only dreams of 'soap operas' plot.

Marvin: "Let's turn off the TV and go upstairs baby girl. I want to make love to you and envelope your soulful desires." Taking her by the hand, he lifts her up into his strong arms, and carries her up the stairs into the bedroom. He lays her upon the bed, and sits next to her, rubbing her temples, slowly moves across her face down to her neck, then to both shoulders, taking a few seconds to relieve tension built up; as he then moves down to both arms, lifting them above her head to expose the upper body. He removes her blouse, the bra and begins to massage the upper body. Afterwards, he moves down and takes off her panties... all the while she lays there with eyes closed – stilled by his touch... his hands then takes one leg and massages it top to bottom, and then the other leg repeating the same, as he then removes his tee shirt and pajama bottom....

Papa West: 'All day and night and still no rats! Shit! Cocked and Loaded and nothing to shoot! Nare rabbit, rat or snake –

not even a stray dog – I'm going to bed. Such a warm night, might as well sleep on the porch, here, let me put my gun next to me in case one of them rats try and eat my foot; I'll blow his little head off!' Moving from the chair to the wicker bench which had a very soft cushion, he covered himself with his light wool blanket and slept.

Marvin: After making love, he sat up against the head board and made a statement. "Listen baby girl; I have some things on my mind that, I want your opinion on."

Pauline: Thinking he was about to mention her cheating on him – she sat up next to him to take her punishment – her heart had just been moved, by the love they had made in such a long while, that she deserved a slap or two for her actions. "Yes baby; I'm ready, go ahead and do it!"

Marvin: "Do What! No, I just want to get your reaction on an idea I want to implement. I want to amass as much money within the next three or four years, to sell my portion of this farm and take my money and purchase some land in California. There I can have two harvests per year. I was looking at one farm which the owner is having problems with getting loans – which I will not have to do – I can get this land for almost nothing. He is asking Seven Hundred Thousand – but, I might be able to get it cheaper if I come with straight cash in hand. It will be a great new start for the both of us – knowing how our marriage has suffered these past few years, because of all the work I'm carrying on my shoulders. Jason has nothing to offer but criticism, and frankly I'm tired of hearing it. Let him take the load and see if he can run and keep this land in his family. The time has come for my family – both present and past – finally get our forty acres and a mule. So, tell me what you think?"

Looking Marvin in his face, and hoping inside he is not just talking – she sits up on her knees, straddles him and inserts herself, and voices what she had for a very long time been wanting to say.

Pauline: "I am ready to follow you to China if that is where you want to start a new life away from this family. This would be the completion of a dream I've waited to come true since we first met. Yes, let's do this together – I will help you anyway you need me to do – do not hesitate to ask me Marvin, I will jump high from this day forward to make sure you are successful. Now, enough talk; let's make a family!"

A cross breeze blows into the room; out the other window as the night is lit only by a half moon, the stars many in the sky, traveling towards the middle of town. There the breeze blows into the window, awaking Jason as it brushes across his face.

Jason: "Uh what, what, why's the bed so small! Oh; these two bitches besides me, that's why? What time is it; where's my phone?"

Mary: "What you say sweetheart?"

*Jason: "I'm not talking to you bitch! I'm speaking out loud –
you see my phone? Oh, there it is over there. The time is…. oh,
it's just 3:45 a.m. – where's that bitch at?"*

*Jane: "We're here in the bed Jason – now, come on back to bed
now, it's getting cold. Close the windows a little bit okay
Jason!"*

*Jason: "I'm not talking about you bitch; I'm talking about that
nigger bitch – she should've been here by now – and, you two
bitches got to go! Get your ass up, get dressed and take your
stank ass home – here, here's two hundred for the both of you.
Nice when I knew you but now, get your asses out!"*

*Getting up from the bed, both women took turns showering
before getting dress to leave. They took up their money,
waved bye to Jason and left. A sense of loneliness had
overcome Jason for a second; making him shiver as though a
winter breeze brushed over him. He turned off the lights and
got back in bed. Trying to go back to sleep, he thought only
about the whereabouts of Pauline. Had Marvin caught her
leaving the house and fought her; or, did she forget that the
two of them were meeting for another short night of good
times. 'Yeah, she must've forgotten our meeting tonight.
Anyway, I'll see her tomorrow when I get back to the farm –
this is the third week since planting them plants and applying
that fertilizer – I have to see just how well the stuff is working.
Let me get some more sleep.'*

Waleed Yaser

Marvin: "Did you sleep well baby girl? Here, I've brought you a glass of water – one needs to stay hydrated especially after sex – so, drink this and go back to sleep."

Pauline: "What time is it Marvin?" Raising herself up and resting on her elbow, she drank the glass of water and handed it back to him.

Marvin: "The time is now 4:25 a.m. – the sun will be up in about an hour, so I wanted to get a head start on the sun – they say it's going to be a hot one today. I have to water the field today – no rain is expected for the next three days, so, I'll bring out the water tank and do the south, east and west ends. Jason doesn't want me near the north end for any reason – and he's made that quite clear. Just last week; I asked if he wanted me to water the north end, and he went berserk on me – telling me not to go in the area, that, he would be the one to care for that section, and I should keep my nose out of his business. Hell, just wanted to water the area. Anyway I'll keep to caring for these other areas and leave him to his little experiment. Okay, I have to go get things moving for the day – I probably won't be ready for lunch till well past 2 p.m. – I'll call you when I need the lunch delivered to me okay." Leaning over to kiss his wife, Marvin walked out the room with a smile on his face. Pauline also had a smile on her face, as she laid back down to sleep.

BOOM! The sound of a shotgun going off early in the morning only meant that, Papa West had just killed something or maybe had a misfire while dropping the gun.

Pauline: "Old man; what the hell are you shooting at this early in the morning? You want the Mexican girls to become frighten, thinking you out to chase them back across the border!"

Papa West: "I got one – finally got one of them damn rats! How soon before breakfast is ready – you is cooking pancakes this morning right? Make me about three with lots of Maple Syrup and butter…."

Pauline: "Now you know the doctor said you shouldn't have too much fat; so, butter is not on your menu. You want decaf coffee with cream or black?"

Papa West: "No butter; well, black with three sugars and hurry it up okay!"

Bring out the tray for him to eat on – the Mexican girl placed before him a short stack of pancakes with a nobb of butter hidden underneath the bottom pancake. She smiled at him and walked back into the house. Pauline came out to make sure he was happy with breakfast. She stood over Papa West, and whispered something in his ear.

Papa West: "What you say girl; I didn't hear you?"

23

Pauline: "I said old man; that, I'm going to take your advice and leave Jason alone. My husband and I are all good and want to start all over again. I will tell Jason when I see him that it's not going to happen anymore between us again. He'll understand and probably curse me out a little but, he'll get over it."

Papa West: "Good for you and Marvin girl – now, go bring me another two pancakes – have that Mexican girl bring it to me; I think she likes me."

Pauline: "She'll put a hurting on you old man – you better leave her alone if you want to see tomorrow – is that all you want for now?" Papa West just waved his hand as to say; 'yes but hurry with them pancakes'.

The Mexicans Jason had hired were already in the fields with rakes and hoes cleaning out the weeds and keeping the topsoil fresh.

Jaime: "Es curioso cómo estas plantas crecen muy rápido. El uso de algo no es bueno para la tierra." (It's funny how these plants grow very fast. He using something no good for the earth.) They all knew something was wrong in these fields, but what was it; some evil spirit evolved in making these plants grow so fast – in just four weeks, they were more than twenty inches high. " Escuche que mantener nuestras bocas cerradas y sólo el trabajo. Nadie dice nada acerca de las plantas." (Listen we keep our mouths closed and just work. No one say anything about the plants.)

It was well after 2 p.m. when Jason arrived to the field. Jamie and the others had completed the cleanup of most of the field, and were soon to finish. Jason had brought a Keg of beer with him for the men to drink in this hot sun.

Jason: "Great job men; here, enjoy this for the afternoon – find a tree and sit under it – I'll finish up here okay. I want to water the fields – so, make yourselves scarce while I go get the water tank."

Jaime and the others grabbed up the heavy keg and made their way more than half a mile away from the fields. Finding a large Oak tree towards the boundary line of the property, they took the remaining hours off under the cool shade and drank half a keg.

Jason drove back to the barn; entering and heading towards the back where the fertilizer was, he tore open another bag and began weighing the contents before placing them into the emptied water tank. 'He wrote, Twenty pounds per hundred gallons of water. Well, I'm not going to follow those instructions anymore. Instead of twenty pounds per hundred gallons , I'm going to put fifty pounds per hundred gallons and see what happens. If this application of fertilizer makes them plants grow any faster than they already are; then, I'm going all out with this first harvest.' Adding a whole bag and a half to the water tank, Jason went about filling the tank with water. It would take up to almost one hour to put three hundred gallons of water in the tank. He would then drive it to the north end of the farm and start spraying the fertilizer over the plants.

Making sure not to run over the growing plants, he took his time going over the whole north end. He finished well after sunset, but not too dark as to drive over all the plants. Jason was driving back to the barn, when he passed by Marvin who, was driving all the workers back into town on the bus.

Jason: "Hey Marv; how many Mexicans you got working for you? Are you paying them good right. Just don't break our budget for this month on that many workers – you can do better with half the amount – we'll talk when you get back okay!"

Marvin: 'That man has too much shit with him! Yeah, we'll talk when I get back; I'll put a foot in his ass. Anyway, I'm getting these fields ready for when the crop sprayer comes next week to lay down the fertilizer. I have all the irrigation setup and ready to go when the plane comes, and, if everything goes as planned, we'll be profiting quite an amount of cash in a few months. This is going to be a good year for the West Farms. Might even setup the road side stands again. Haven't done that in a few years now – hell, might even give Papa something to do, instead of sitting all day holding that shot gun. "Okay everybody – you all get out at Main Street and I'll pick you up tomorrow at 7 a.m. sharp."

Jason: "Hey Pauline! Pauline! Come out back for a minute!" Peering into the kitchen window as Pauline and the two girls cooked for the twelve people staying at the farm, he knew this was the best time to speak with her, with Marvin dropping off the workers in town.

Pauline knew she had to tell Jason that their affair was now and forever over. The timing was right, with Marvin in town dropping off the workers, she would make it clear to Jason not to ever cross that line again.

Pauline: "Yeah Jason; what do you want? And make it quick, I have much to do tonight before dinner is served."

Jason: "I missed you at the bungalow the other night. What happen, why didn't you come?"

Pauline: "Listen Jason; this is it between you and I – I mean, we won't be having sex together anymore. I'm making things better with Marvin, and we've got plans for our future. Hell, I might even have a baby now- who would've thought that – me having a baby! Well, we're going to try very hard together; and you no longer are invited. It was nice while it lasted, but things change and I have changed Jason. I hope you understand!"

Jason: "So, you're going to live with that boring ass man – who thinks nothing else but farming – that's not what you need Pauline. You need a man to show you affection and tell you things in your ear to make you feel like a real woman. Will Marvin do that for you? No, I don't think he has it in him. Anyway, it's no skin off my back if you want to end it – but, trust me, you'll be visiting my bungalow again, just watch, and I'll not answer that door when that time comes. I'm replacing you with a newer and less traveled model."

Pauline: "Okay; are you finished? Anyway Jason you take care of yourself alright. Don't bring home any disease that can't be thrown back. Dinner will be ready in thirty minutes; now, go clean up and come to the table." Walking back into the back door to the kitchen, she continued to roll out the biscuits as the girls worked on the meat and potatoes part of the dinner.

Jason: "I'm not eating here tonight; I'm going to Henderson NC for the next few days. Tell Marvin to watch my men and make sure they work. I've paid them for the week so, he doesn't have to bother with that. See you when I see you!" Getting into his Corvette and heading towards the main gate, he passes by Marvin who was just returning from the city. Not acknowledging Marvin; he drove past and head towards North Carolina.

DAY THREE IN N.C.

Jamie: "Este es el diablo de trabajo esta finca y no voy a quedarme más tiempo de trabajo para el Sr. Jason. Todos tenemos que salir antes de que seamos convocados por el mismo diablo. Sr. Jason puede mantener su dinero. Ven conmigo los hombres nos vamos ahora para casa, México nos espera, y nuestras familias nos aman mucho a compartir con el diablo". ("This is the devil working this farm and I will not stay longer work for Mr. Jason. All we have to go before we are summoned by the devil himself. Mr. Jason can keep your money. Come with me, men we go now to home, Mexico is waiting for us and our families love us a lot to share with the devil. ") Jamie and the other five men left the farm without telling anyone. It began when the six of them woke up as they had done for the month and twenty days of working for Jason; that when they entered upon the north end, they were astonished by what they saw. Just the day before, the stalks of corn were no higher than thirty-six inches. But, here this morning they have grown to be more than six feet tall and full of corn. This couldn't be anything but the work of evil, and so, they decided to leave before anything else happened.

That night a light rain fell upon the farm. It was needed as the remaining farm had now begun to flourish all over. Marvin had done a great job cultivating and cleaning the rows of vegetables, that, it was surely going to be a profitable year. This was sure to help in his future goals of leaving this land and getting his own. He was sure to stay clear of the north end as Jason had asked. If Jason was going to fail he would accomplish that on his own.

Marvin: "Just look out the window baby girl. You see our future growing beautifully on the land. We'll have our own place quicker than we thought. If we have another year like this one, we'll reach our goal within two years."

Pauline: "I'm happy for you baby! But what do you think about Jason. Do you think he'll buy your portion of the farm from you? He could low ball you and force you to take a very low price. It's all up to whether he will oblige us and let us go."

Marvin: "I'm not worried about what he thinks baby girl. The land will speak for itself as far as being profitable for the both of us. He most likely will lose this farm in two or three years anyway. He has no desire to care and cultivate this land as a mother cares and cultivates her new born child. No, he'll purchase my portion – I bet my life on it. By the way; I haven't seen him in four days now – he still in North Carolina right?"

Pauline: "When he left here, that's where he said he'd be for a few days. As a matter of fact; I haven't seen his workers the past two day either. Is something going on around here, that, we don't know anything about? You want to go take a look at the north end and see if you see his workers?"

Marvin: "No baby girl I don't! He asked me to stay away, so, I will stay away from whatever he is doing over there. As long as he puts in his part of the harvest we have no problem with him. Whether he plays all night and sleeps all day, it's all about what we bring to the market come that time. He said he had it under control, then I will leave him to his word. You feel like going into town and catching a movie. The girls can watch Papa West – he's hooked on one of them anyway – maybe he'll put down that shot gun and have fun with them for the evening. I'll take out his John Wayne movies for him – you go get ready alright."

Girl: "Stop touching me you dirty old Gringo! Now sit down and watch the movie. You want me to make some more tacos for you?"

Papa West: "Yeah, make as many as you like my hot pepper – but who'll fix this damn movie. I never seen John Wayne speak Spanish before. This damn DVD isn't working right."

Girl: "Nothing is wrong with the movie old man – it's just that we like him too and want to hear it in our language – you know this movie too well, so, not having English won't spoil the movie for you."

Papa West: "You girls hear that? Sounds like my grandson's car coming down the path. Wait, let me take a look. Yeah, it's his car alright – boys been gone for almost a week – wonder who he knocked up this time! Hurry up with them tacos and, them nachos baby! Ha ha ha! "

Parking the Corvette in the garage – Jason walked into the barn to get an update from Jamie. Once inside, he noticed how dark and quiet the barn was. Walking towards the workers quarters, he knocked on the door and opened it. It was dark so he turned on the light. There was no one in the room, not one bed had been slept in. The room was clean as it was when he first brought them here.

Jason: 'Where these wet-backs go? They left and didn't take care of my land – shit, they'll have hell to pay for if it is ruined. Let me drive down to the north end and see what's been done these past four days.' Getting into the pickup and heading towards the north end to inspect his crops. He could see from the lights that everything looked well, the stalks were almost seven feet tall, and full of large heads of corn. His heart raced as he got closer and closer. This stuff really worked and it work wonderfully. He felt secured in knowing that he'd get two harvests from this land this year. If the other workers walked off leaving all this corn on the stalk, he'd find others to replace them, just to get this stuff to the market.

Here he was already going to take roughly four or five bushels of corn to the market and get paid well for it. He thought to himself, that he'd plant the next crop the following week and this time increase the amount of fertilizer to four times the amount per hundred gallons. Oh, how he relished this very moment. But, there behind those stalks – there seemed to be a bald spot in the field that hadn't grown anything. It was just bare dirt like nothing had germinated at all. What was the problem – why wouldn't this one spot yield to him corn like the rest of this area. He needed to know whether or not Marvin had come down here and gotten jealous, seeing how prosperous his fields were. 'That asshole; he'd better not had done anything to my field, when I told him not to come here and touch it – I'm sure he did something. I'll find out when I get back to the house.'

Driving like a crazy man down the dirt road, Jason pulled up to the back of the house. He entered the back door to the kitchen and walked into the media room, where Papa West and the two girls were watching the movie.

Jason: "Where's Marvin; is he here Papa!" Standing before them was this face of an devil or one about to become the devil.

Papa West: "What's the problem here boy! Why you want to go mess up my movie with these girls – what you want Marvin for! He isn't here; he's at the movies with his wife. Now, get out before I shoot you for being stupid."

Jason: "He'd done gone and messed up my crops Papa!"

Papa West: "What you say boy! He isn't done nothing of the sort – he ain't been on the north end all week, and I've been out there in my chair all day and night; you know how I am, can't sleep till sunrise. No son; it not Marvin I can vouch for that in court. Maybe it was them there Mexicans you hire who destroyed your crops; not Marvin! Now, what happened – tell me what they did!"

Jason: "Nothing Papa; don't worry about it. I just got my under wears on too tight or something. I know what to do – I'll take care of fixing the crops. When Marvin gets in tell him to call me on my cell phone okay Papa!"

Papa West: "Yeah boy go on now! Leave me to these girls here! Give me another one of the tacos girl."

Walking off Jason was determined to fix that one small spot. He would gather up some seeds and mix a very strong fertilizer mix to pour over the new seeds. They would sure start to grow by morning time. He would add ten pounds to just twenty gallons of water and pour it over the newly planted seeds. He would then head back to the barn and return all the equipment and then make his way to bed. On his way to the house, he heard Marvin's voice as he a Papa spoke about him.

Marvin: Papa West; you know me better than that. You know I would never sabotage Jason's work – I try to encourage him, but he's not interested in wanting to learn how to run a farm. I swear on Great grand pappy West's head; that I had nothing to do with his north end. Listen, I'm going to bed now. If Jason wants to talk to me about it, we can talk and I'll also mention to him that I want to sell my part of the land to him. I'm finished with this Papa West; and when I leave, I'm taking you with me. Jason will never look after you like I would. Okay; we'll talk in the morning. Night Papa West – get some sleep okay!"

Jason listened until he heard Marvin's bedroom door close. Walking to the guest house, he entered and laid down on his bed. He knew Marvin too well to know he wasn't telling the truth – especially when he swore on Great grand pappy – because he too was his relative! If he didn't do it, then it must've been them Mexicans that did it and then ran off. He'd catch up to them someday; but, for now he needed to sleep. He would get up early to head back to the north end to see if he could figure out what happen.

As he dreamt about all that corn growing; one thing kept sticking itself into that dream. There was this very old woman crying about how they have soiled her and poison her for all these years and that, she would take her revenge against all who hurt her. And when the old lady said that, she would look at Jason and point her finger. The dream would repeat itself all night long. Jason knew he done nothing to an old lady to want her revenge against him. Surely she was mistaken and he would explain to her it is not him who hurt her. But still the dream continued until he awoke wet from sweat or was it.

Jason: 'Sick ass dream boy. What old lady have you hurt in your life – none but young ladies have been used by me – but an old lady; no not you Jason!' "Okay get up take a shower and get out to the field. I've got to figure out what happen so the next crop won't repeat itself." Upon arriving at the north end, Jason took out his rake and shovel and walked over to the patch in the ground. Looking at it revealed nothing special in the sunlight. Even where Jason planted the seed the night before showed not even one seed in the hole. Something was *not right in London. Taking the rake, he scratched at the soil, which seemed to be soft and rich in color.*

"DIG UP THE SOIL IT IS NO GOOD!"

Jason: "Who's there? Show yourself!" 'Must be tripping out – might be the after affects of all that drug and drinking in N. C. – anyway, the soil smells normal. Even with all that fertilizer I put on it last night, nothing seems to be wrong with…..' "Hello; is there anyone there?" Climbing up onto the back of the pickup, looking all around, seeing nothing, he knew he was going batty for sure. "Listen, if you're out there just reveal yourself – maybe I can give you some work – or maybe you're lost and need a ride. No problem, just show yourself!" Climbing back down and walking over to the shovel, he dug it into the ground and started taking out the soil. For the next two hours he dug the ground looking for reason why this soil won't germinate. Jason continued until he had to climb out of the hole. "I need a ladder!" Driving back to the barn, Jason sees Marvin heading out towards the west end of the farm. He couldn't hear Jason pull up because of the Tractor engine. He entered the barn and carried out the ten foot ladder. This was long enough to climb up and down without any difficulty. Arriving back to the hole, Jason noticed that some of the dirt had fallen back into the hole. He would spend the next three hours digging and digging – like he was possessed by something – but dig he did until he was exhausted and sweaty. He had dug almost seven feet down and didn't realize it until some dirt from above fell upon his face. Climbing out, he heard again a sound like someone speaking – but from where did this sound originate – he couldn't locate it or who might be calling out. It was just at that very moment, that a sound came from below. A rock had fallen back into the hole, and the sound of metal was heard below.

Jason: "What is that down there?" Climbing back down the ladder, he took the shovel and continued to dig. Another sound of metal against metal was detected. What is buried under this soil – maybe it's the reason nothing grows here – maybe it's a box or even a buried treasure or something that Great grand pappy buried for us to find in the future. It was said that he was very rich at one time before the Civil War started. Maybe he buried his riches here for safe keeping until the South won the war. But when the North won; he knew they'd take everything he owned, so, he left it buried for his kin to find. That's it; it's got to be all the gold and silver he was said to have had. Just dig a bit more out….yes, it is a metal box or something like a box. "Shit! This boy is rich – I found the buried treasure – shut the hell up boy; you want everybody to hear you. Get your ass out of this hole and go and get that Nigger relative out of the ownership – you can't share this finding with him or even Papa West. Marvin said he did want to sell his part of the farm; well, I'll make him an offer he won't refuse. I got to get back and call my lawyer and the bank officer. I need to see how much this property is worth, and how soon I can get the paper written up to purchase Marvin's part of the farm."

Climbing out of the hole and dusting himself off; Jason got into the pickup and headed back to the house. Driving like a bat out of hell, he parked near the back door and ran upstairs to his room in the guest house. There in the closet in a shoe box, was the deed to the farm. It listed his Great Great Grandfather and Marvin's Great Great Grandfather the freed slave.

Taking the deed in hand, he ran down the stairs to the pickup and called his lawyer first and then the bank. His lawyer would start on the papers as soon as he got back in town from Canada. The banker had given him a two million dollar credit on the land which was worth six plus million. He would then take the deed and head into the house. There, he saw Pauline with the two Mexican girls cooking up a storm. Sitting on the porch in his usual spot, was Papa West with his shot gun in his lap.

Jason: "Pauline; call Marvin and ask him to come to the house as quick as he can. Tell him I have a proposition for him to decide whether he wants his dream to start now or later."

Pauline: "What's going on here Jason; are you alright?"

Jason: "Never felt better Pauline. What do you have heated up to eat?"

Pauline: "There are some home fries and Chicken fried steak there if you want them. They are still warm – here, let me get you a plate."

Jason: "Call Marvin and get him here now; I'm very busy and I have to finish before dark. You got any buttermilk in the house – steak and buttermilk go good together."

Girl: "Si se`nor there is buttermilk for you. Let me fill your glass for you."

Pauline: "He's on his way Jason. Are you sure you're alright – you look a little pale, like you're coming down with something?"

Jason: "No, I'm just fine! Never felt better in my life as I do now – these home fries are good but, the steak is a bit tough to eat. Anyway thanks for the food. How soon before Marvin gets here – seems like hours have gone by – oh, I see him now pulling up near the barn. I'll meet him outside – thanks Pauline!" Running out the kitchen door across the driveway, Jason stood face to face with Marvin.

Jason: "Listen Marvin; I want to make you an offer for your third of this land. I know you are looking to move on to something of your own, so, let me help you in your endeavor. Just how much would you want for your third of this land?"

Listening to his Jason's sincerity in his voice, he knew he was not joking. Was this a dream or a nightmare coming? He didn't have an idea of what this property was really worth, but he would throw out a number and see if it stuck.

Marvin: "What say we start at one and a half million dollars? Can you come up with that kind of money?"

Jason: "That's a good starting point Marvin. I was looking at let's say; one million dollars – but, if an extra half million is going to make this deal go quicker, then let's make this deal. I can have my lawyer draw up the papers as soon as he's back in town, which should be in a day or two. So, we have a deal right? Let's shake on it Marvin!" Holding out his hand to seal the deal, Marvin took hold.

Marvin: "It's a deal Jason! But, I will be taking Papa West with me when I leave. You can never take care of the man in the right way."

Jason: "Deal; take the old fool – he doesn't really like me anyway! Okay, I will be in touch with you in a few days. Also, the harvest to come will belong to me – I will give you a percentage for all the work you've done so far. Let's say we add an extra two hundred thousand to the final offer, which makes it one point seven million. Okay that it and I'm out of here – see you in the lawyers office."

Marvin turned and walked back towards the house. Something just wasn't right with what just went down. It was too easy and no haggling from Jason – it's not like him to just hand over money like that – he had something up his sleeve and Marvin wanted to know what it was. 'I got to tell Pauline and Papa

West what just happened. Maybe they can put a finger on what might be happening here. Anyway; I rid myself of this headache and of him especially. I can head out to California and purchase that land I was praying to get; but, now I get it much earlier than I thought.' "Hey baby girl; you'll never guest what just happen. We're moving to the land of sunshine and beaches!"

Driving like a mad man possessed; Jason drove up to the patch of dirt and climbed down the hole. Grabbing the shovel again, he began digging up more dirt to expose the item buried. It took another twenty minutes before he could see what exactly was buried. 'A Door! What the hell is this – who'd burry a metal door this deep underground?' Taking the shovel he slammed it hard down on top of the door to dislodge it. He stood there hitting it over and over again, until he heard something that made him scurry out of that hole.

Jason: "What the Fuck was that? Whose voice is that – sounds like a woman's voice – shit man, what's going on here?" Looking down into the hole he stood watching, waiting to hear if the voice would answer again. "This is a trip! I got to go get someone to witness this with me – no one would believe me if I was ever to tell them what what…. what happening now?"

To his amazement the door began to open. Looking attentively at what might come out of that door Jason was frozen and couldn't move. The door opened widely and there below him was this figure.

I AM MOTHER EARTH AND THIS IS SATAN HIMSELF – WE INVITE YOU TO JOIN US BECAUSE YOU HAVE POISIONED THIS SOIL AND DISRESPECTED THIS EARTH FOR FAR TOO LONG. COME IN AND FEEL THE FIRE FOREVER LONG AS THIS EARTH EXISTS!

Jason's face was as pale as snow – as the flames rushed upwards at him and engulfs his whole body and returned into the hole. There only stood his bones as they too fell within the hole. The sound of the door slamming shut was heard about as the birds flew from their nest in mass numbers. Slowly the dirt dug out of the hole fell back in and filled itself.

There rising amongst the soil was on lone sprout shut green and tall! Looking into the window, and setting on top of the dashboard of the pickup truck was, the deed to the farm. Upon looking at it closely, one could see Jason's signature written, where it would be when transferring the property over. It now showed that Marvin West was sole proprietor to said land. Somehow in his haste to get this deal done, he signed in the wrong place – or, were there some sinister powers in control of this matter – even though, all was legal and binding in any Court. This entire farm was now the sole ownership to Marvin West.

In the coming weeks, as they sought to iron out this transfer in the City Court House; the search for Jason was now officially a recovery operation by the State Police. No foul play was ever *discovered in or around the farm – and the Mexicans who had worked for him were also interviewed and who had alibis, having all six being jailed for drunk and disorderly chargers. Jason's whereabouts were a mystery.*

Papa West: "Well, now that we own this land Marvin, what will you do now? You aren't going to sell it to one of the Corporate Supermarket chains, are you? Or bring in a developer to build many multi-million dollar homes – like I've seen done elsewhere in South Carolina, are you boy? Tell me exactly what you have planned for this land your Great, great grandfather once slaved on, I want to know?"

Marvin: "Well, Papa West let me first tell you what I will do. I'm going to adjoin the guest house to the main house, where we can have a nursery close to our Master Bedroom. Then after that, I'm going to renovate the porch so it can be weatherize for uses all year long. Which means; that you can sit out there in your chair even when the snow is falling – it'll be nice, warm and cozy for you no matter what. Then, have a small bed and breakfast built just over there with a pool for the hot summers. This way Pauline can make an income for herself – she loves these two Mexican girls, so, maybe she'll find a place in the guest house for their families to come and live. We have a lot of work to do, in order to bring this farm up to 21th Century standards."

Papa West: "Yeah sonny it sure does. Then, I guess you have to get started hiring people to work this farm. We are soon to harvest the crops you planted – but, tell me something."

Marvin: "What's that Papa West? What do you want to know?"

Papa West: "The north end where Jason planted all that corn. What will you do with all of it? You are going to sell it to them people who make ethanol?"

Marvin: No, Papa West I'm not! When I found the fertilizer in the barn which Jason used, and all the chemicals which were composed of this product, I burnt it and will likewise do the same to the north end. I'm going to burn it all down to the ground and start over. Hopefully, the soil is not contaminated from the fertilizer, and that I can raise a new crop before the season ends. One idea I have is to turn the north end into a fruit bearing section only. Like maybe I'll plant some apple trees or even peaches – how does that sound Papa West – you can have fresh fruit whenever you want."

Papa West: "Nah; I like Strawberries – or let's say Blueberries – yeah we'll plant them!"

Marvin: "Anything you want Papa West; anything you want! Now, let's go eat. Pauline is waiting for us!"

Pulling back as the two walk into the farmhouse we see just how beautiful this farm land really is. There on the north end, we view three men; small figures whom are setting aflame to the corn.   Fade Out!

Waleed Yaser

ARTHUR AVENUE DEAD END!

Waleed Naeem Yaser
December 22, 2011

Waleed Yaser

Way back in the 1990's when life on the streets was rough and only the tough were able to move about with impunity. Many blocks were monitored by hand men, who would fist fight at the drop of a hat. Every corner in the city had groups of gangs that were like little corporations. There were; Drugs, Prostitution, Racketeering and even Executions if the price was right.

One such street in the Bronx; of the city of New York, was Arthur Avenue. The gang was known as the Napoli Boyz. They ran the street from Fordham Road to East Tremont Avenue; three to five gangs of Italian descent. On the other side of Fordham Road by Webster Avenue, roamed a Afro American gang called the Black Dragons, who sold Drugs and stolen Auto parts to international dealers.

Every now and then, both groups would cross fist at the White House Burger joint on Fordham Road. At one such crossing; both girls and boys of teen age would square off in the parking lot and see who was best in fists battle. That night Jeffery had his gang from Webster standing around while he fought with Vito from Arthur Avenue. Both were giving and taking; blood was drawn on both side and the crowd cheered them on.

It was the arrival of the New York City Police which broke up the crowd, causing the many to scatter and return to their blocks. As Jeffery ran to the other side of Fordham Road, he looked back and noticed Vito's girl smiling back at him. He returned the smile and ran towards Webster Avenue. She then gripped Vito's shirt collar and straighten it.

Jenna: "You really put it to him this time Vito. He's bleeding more than you are. Here, let me clean your cheek with my handkerchief."

Vito: "Yeah baby; I put something on his ass tonight! Even his own boys know he got his ass handed to him. I should've knocked his ass out right there at White House. Next time I meet him will hopefully be his last! His time is over for running that gang – he's getting soft in the pants – maybe we'll even expand our territory towards Webster Avenue."

Jenna: "Uh um Vito you're right; the toughest always take over the weakest territory." 'Yeah but, you got your ass handed to you by Jeffery. He went easy on your ass.' "How about eating some Cannoli's and Coffee at Artie's Café Vito?"

Walking back down Arthur Avenue; Jenna thoughts were strictly on Jeffery. He had caught her eye, when she thought he'd really hurt Vito; and let up on him for the duration of the fight. She saw in his eyes something that said... 'we can exist together on these blocks' – maybe even he was tired of all the fighting between the Italian's and Afro American – but would

3

she put herself out there to find out. That night she would make her mind up to secretly meet with him; but how would she get this message to him.

Die B: "You went easy on that votto back there Jeffery, why?"

Jeffery: "I don't really know bro; but, I felt sorry for his silly ass, thinking he could go with me. Plus, his girl looked at me with concern for him and I got soft I guess! Anyway, we let them know they just can't bull guard the whole parking lot at White House Burgers. It belongs to us just as much as it belongs to them."

Die B: "Then, why not set up boundaries between us in the parking lot. There are two large sections of the parking lot that the two of us can occupy without having to fight every other night. We got too much business going on here to be having to go to the jail or the hospitals. I know some in our gang don't like hearing this type of talk, but I'm not just speaking semantics here; I want us to make money and all this fighting brings the Po Po down on us too often. You know they won't go mess with them Italians boys and ruffle up their money flow, so why ours? I think we need to have a parlay between the top tiers among us."

Jeffery: "I can go along with that Die B – but, who'll make the first request for a truce between us – neither you nor I will be listened to. Anyway, let us try to get this done."

Weeks went by and nothing got done. The tension at the White House Burger continued to simmer as both groups went and came for sliders and fries. It was then that a messenger from a suspicious point of view came up to Jeffery. It was Hector the Drunk; and he'd been told not to hang out around the kids here at the park. He was only allowed in after dark, when all the kids were home.

Jeffery looked at him walking through the gate, pass the swings and slide, over to the table where Die B and him sat talking.   What did he have in his hands beside the beer bottle?

Die B: "What you want in this park Hector! You've been told not to come here during the day, now, what is it?"

Hector: "This White Chick gave me this letter to give to Jeffery; that's all and I'll leave when I do. Oh; Die B! Can you give me a nickel for a three piece chicken lunch? I'll clean up the park tonight when I'm finish okay?" Handing the letter to Jeffery; he took the five dollars from Die B and walked out the other end of the park and down to Hassan's Chicken Hut!

Die B: "What's it say Jeffery – who wrote it?"

Looking at the penmanship said it was a woman for sure. But which woman would use Hector to delivery it – any of the other sisters would send one of the kids around here. Reading it he knew who might've sent it when he got to the last few words. 'When our eyes met I felt something I've yet to

5

experience. I saw your feeling were exposed as mines were for just a few seconds, so I needed to contact you by any means that I could without stirring up anymore problems with us. It is time we stopped hurting each other Jeffery and co-exist. I want you to meet me tomorrow night at the Bronx Zoo under path near the parking lot. Come alone as I too will be alone! Come at midnight; Italian Jenna!'

Jeffery: "Uh, just a babe that's all! She says she has the hot pants and wants to get with me."

Die B: "She got any girlfriends – want me to hang with you, or you doing this by yourself?"

Jeffery: "I'm skating on this ice alone bro! I'll let you know how things turned out."

Die B: "Are you going to meet her tonight?"

Jeffery: "Naw not tonight; tomorrow night at midnight. I'll give you the lowdown if she has a girl for you alright. If she does, maybe we'll hang out at the movies on Forty-Second Street. Come on let's get back to business. Now, you have four cars staked out in Mount Vernon near Bronxville. Two Mercedes, a Jaguar and a Beemer! Good, we'll take all four tonight! Go get the guys and meet me at my house alright!"

The night was a very successful venture for them. Not only did they get the four cars, but things turned out to very profitable. The organization out of Brighten Beach Brooklyn paid very handsomely for each car. The Russian boss handed them a list of cars they would need to have for him at the end of the month. It was an average of two cars per day; with a pay out of ten grand for each car. All were high end vehicles ranging from Sixty Thousand to over a Hundred Thousand.

The Russians were shipping them back home and making a mock up of over thirty thousand each car. So, if the car was worth eighty grand, they sell it for fifty, after paying the Black Dragons ten grand. That was roughly over a hundred and forty thousand per week if they could keep up with the quota. The following day, which was the night he would meet with Jenna, he sent out his crew to Connecticut for two cars. He would wait until 11 p.m. to make sure the cars were delivered to the Russian, before taking his shower and dressing for the evening.

 RING RING RING The phone rang as he was showering, running naked into his bedroom, he answered it. It was Die B telling him of the money was paid and they were on their way back uptown.

Jeffery: "Good work Die B; listen, I'll be leaving for my date, so just divide up the cash and bring my split to my house. I'll give you a call sometime in the morning okay. Take care and stay out of trouble!" Dressing in a blue pinstripe leisure suit he made his way towards the Bronx Zoo. It was near twelve when he got there, and she was already there, waiting next to the under path.

Jenna: "I see you made it and you're on time. I was not sure you'd come. I was standing here thinking you wouldn't come. Like maybe I'd set you up or something like that. But, I'm glad you came. Hi; I'm Jenna and I'm happy to meet you." She was of an olive complexion, with streaky blonde and brunette hair, and a body like some sisters. She held out her hand for him to take.

Taking it and kissing it he looked into her eyes to see if she expresses the same sentiments of the night before. Her face glowed in the street lights; as her smile radiated pleasure and tighten grip around his hand.

Jeffery: "I'm Jeffery and it is truly my pleasure to finally meet you Jenna. No, I never thought you do something as silly as set me up. When I looked into your eyes the other night, I saw something most Italian girls don't show to a man like me, when so many people are around. But let's not dwell upon trivial things like that. Let's go for a ride downtown. We'll take a taxi to let's say The Village and walk around until we think of something to do. Maybe take in a movie and then something to eat. I know this cool Pizza Parlor that makes the best pizza in New York. Tell me; how late can you stay out?"

Jenna: "We can watch the sun rise if you want."

These secret rendezvous continued for more than three months. Sometime three times a week, as the two different in culture, race and local were falling in love. Jeffery was a light skin, light brown eyes Afro American with an Afro!

All of this was to come to a stop a while later. While rummaging through a garbage bin behind a restaurant, Hector the drunk had half his body hanging out, when he was grabbed by the legs and pulled to the ground.

Salvatore: "Hey Vito; looks like we caught a 'Spick' eating without paying. What'd think we should do to him; uh, break either his legs or his arms which one?"

There as Hector lay upon the ground looking up at eight Italian boys, with bats and iron rods – waiting to pounce upon him like craze animals. Hector looked scared out of his mind, as he held up his hands hoping to block the first strike. Salvatore took his bat and raised it above his head and was about to take the first hit which was aimed at his legs.

Hector: "Please wait I know something about this Italian girl having sex with a black guy!" The bat slammed down onto his right thigh with a thump! "Ah! No, please stop. I'll tell everything – she even gave me a letter to bring to him – don't hit me anymore, please stop!"

Just when all were about to get involved with the beating; Vito halted the beating! He bent down looking Hector in his face and spoke.

Vito: "What Italian girl are you talking about you half black niggar spick?"

9

Hector: "When she gave me the letter; I read it and delivered it to Jeffery over on Webster Avenue."

Vito: "What did the letter say and what is the girl's name? If you want to walk away from here you better stop stalling and tell us!"

Hector: "She asked him to meet her by the Bronx Zoo and she signed it Jenna!"

All the faces turned pale white from the mentioning of that name. They all looked at Vito with their mouths open, waiting for a response from Vito. Which was; to kill Hector for saying such a lie against his girl, or talking about Italian women, going out with the niggars in the first place.

Jonny: "Well; she hasn't been around with us these past few weeks right Vito. Like she's been spending time with some of the other girls downtown; isn't that what she told you?"

Vito: "Shut your pee hole Jonny; nobody told you to speak! Now spick niggar; tell me what she looked like. And if you're wrong you will be sleeping with the garbage forever. Nobody will miss you nor care if you are living or dead. Now, tell me what she looked like!"

Hector: "Well, she has a body like a Puerto Rican girl with blonde and black hair. I really couldn't tell, because it was dark, you know. Listen, I'm telling you the truth about this, so please don't hurt me anymore."

Salvatore: "Yo Vito; it's her for sure! Your girl is stepping out on you with a Moolie – and this spick knows about it – he'll surely go around talking in the streets about it too. I say we shut his mouth for good!"

Hector: "You promised not to hurt me if I told you the truth!"

Vito: "I lied spick – now, eat all the garbage you like. Finish him boys and dump his ass deep into the dumpster. I don't want his body found for years. Salvatore; come with me and leave the others to get rid of him. We have to check up on that winch Jenna. If she's seeing that niggar it's finished between us, and she'll have to move from our area!"

Hector then received the worst beating a human body could take without falling to pieces. They rapped him in some plastic and stuffed him in a cardboard box and placed him in the bottom of the dumpster. A few days later he was taken to the landfill in Staten Island. Hector the drunk would never be heard of again; but would surely be missed in the neighborhood. The park had gone without cleaning for over three weeks. And it was also during that time that Jeffery received some startling news from Jenna.

The two of them had met in a far off place where they'd not be disturbed – a place where seeing an Italian and Black together wasn't harmful to one's health. They had come to Mount Vernon which was just a #2 Subway train ride away.

Waleed Yaser

Sitting in the bleachers watching the Jamaicans play a game of Soccer, and the many women and men running around the track, they held hands as the evening breeze rushed about the grandstand. It was nearing sunset and they had not really scheduled this date, as they had become use to Friday and Sunday days for meeting. But, Jenna was insistence upon having this meeting so, they met. What she was about to say, would change both of their lives for some time to come.

Jeffery: "Afterwards if you like Jenna, we can take the bus to New Rochelle and have pizza and drinks at this lovely restaurant. Who'd think it was Mexicans making some of the best pizza in this area. So, what has brought us here that we couldn't wait until the weekend to say?"

Jenna sat holding his hands, when the words dribble out of her mouth. At first it seemed to him that she might've miss spoke, but when she repeated it he was sure of their new position together, as such precarious times in their lives would not sustain.

Jeffery: "How many months are you Jenna? What do you want to do; abort it or keep it – whichever decision we make I will stand by you. We can't stay here together and marry – we'd have to leave the Bronx and maybe head into Connecticut, or even down south somewhere. We'll have to really think this one out. So, tell me what you have in mind!"

Jenna just sat there holding his hand, thinking off into the abyss of what life would be like with him and their baby.

Jenna: "I need time before I can make such a decision Jeffery. I am two weeks late so, we are in the early stages, and if we both decide to abort we will. But, if we decide to keep it; then, life together will be heartbreak for both my parents. They will never accept you nor will they own up to me as their child. I will be disowned and forgotten for as long as I live. But, I don't care if I can live my life with you Jeffery. Our baby will be very beautiful or handsome! But you Jeffery will have to change your life style. There will be no more gangs, drugs or anything that will take you away from the two of us – the baby and I – it is now your decision whether you can make such a change in your life. If not; then I say we just end it with aborting the fetus, and we go our separate ways."

Jeffery: "You are really putting the burden on my shoulders Jenna; one that I could make if I really wanted to be with you for all the life I have left. This decision I can make – I can go anywhere in this world and open a automotive repair shop and make a good living. Maybe even do some restorations on older cars too. If we both decide to do this we should give it a try! I have monies stacked away with family members so, getting the cash is not a problem. The problem lies as to where we will start this new life. You think about a state or county were we would be accepted as a couple, and we'll make that move. I can give the business over to Die B to run from here on out. It should take me no more than a month to get everything in order. Okay; let's take the bus to New Rochelle."

Jenna: "Jeffery; once we take these initiatives and put them in motion, there is no stopping them. We will have the baby and get married without my family knowing. I will just disappear and most likely never see them again. Maybe, somewhere down the road, I will try and contact them – but for now I am a albatross a nobody."

The two of them walked off to the bus stop and went to New Rochelle. Following closely behind them in a car, was Vito and Salvatore. Witnessing everything for himself, Vito knew what needed to be done. They would find a way to entrap Jeffery and get rid of him. As for Jenna; she would be banished from Arthur Avenue forever.

SHATTERED GLASS

Weeks had gone by, and Jenna and Jeffery hadn't seen each other, so to keep things under cover. Each was doing their part in preparing the new life they would live together. Jeffery had handed over the car thief business to Die B and the gang. The Russians were making hundreds of thousands each month, and Die B and the gang living large. Jeffery's family had collected all his monies from around the state and he had contacted the Real Estate agent about a Ranch in Enfield Connecticut. All he was waiting for was the Deed to sign and the keys handed over for their occupancy of the property. It seemed the cards had fallen into place and life with Jenna and the baby was now a reality.

Jeffery had gone down to Hunts Point one evening to see about purchasing a Frame straightening machine for his restoration business, when he was confronted by two Italian boys. He noticed they had looked familiar – but from what part of town they came didn't register. Walking more bristly down the street to where he'd parked the car, he was confronted by another group. He turned and headed down this dark street hoping to flank them and get back to where his car was, but still he found himself trapped with nowhere to go but over the fence of a abandon Used Parts business. Once over the fence he ran towards the back of the business, hoping to find another way out. All he found was a twenty foot high wall with barbwire on top to keep out the unwanted. Now, he turned to make beeline back to the front of the yard, only to find they all had climbed over and was looking for him. Heading towards the back of the yard again seeking to find something to throw over the wall and climb up; put him into a corner with no place to go. He turned to face his foes and to take out as many as he could before they took him out.

Jeffery: "Come on boys; come get some of this!" He took out two Jack Knifes holding one as to stab and the other to slash; he stood waiting for the first fool to attack.

Vito: "Finally we have you where we want you Jeffery! We're going to teach you a lesson you'll never forget as long as you live. You should've kept that dick of yours in out of my girlfriend pussy. Jenna was my girl and now you've tainted her forever, no respectful Italian will ever lay with her. I only hope I would've found out about this earlier, I would've done the two of you together while you were screwing. They would have thought a rape gone badly or something like that, but anyway Jeffery, get ready to die."

What they had brought with them was inside three large bags. Jeffery stood near a corner so as not to allow anyone to get behind him. The sun had set and darkness was growing upon them. All Jeffery could see were glistening glass bottles, most likely beer bottles. What were they going to do with them; he didn't know until he heard one break and then smash against the wall behind him. Then he heard many being broke and thrown in his direction. He held his arms up to block them, but the sharp edges sliced into his skin. When he tried to run over to the other side of the wall, glass bottles followed his every move. Looking around for a shield or something to block the bottles was futile. The bottles was hitting him over his entire body – all he could do was to cover his face, in hopes that when they found his body, his mother could have an open coffin. He took the thrashing for what seemed an hour but in reality, it only took ten minutes for all the bottles to be finished.

Walking up to Jeffery as he laid upon the ground bleeding from every part of his body, Vito stood over him and gave the last warning he'd hear for some time to come.

Vito: "A lesson learnt by the professor of death. Now, you and Hector the Puerto Rican spick will be sleeping together in Hell. You should've stayed on your side of the corner Jeffery. I pray the last thing you see before dying is Jenna's face. See you in Hell Niggar!" Vito and his boys climbed back over the fence and made their way back to Arthur Avenue.

 Jeffery would lay bleeding for over four hours, until a passing dog with his master – who having a flashlight - noticed his moaning from behind the fence. Police were called and the gate cut open; there they would find Jeffery half dead and in a Coma. He would be rushed to Jacoby Hospital and placed in the IC (intensive care) unit. His family would be contacted and they would spend the next three days sleeping in the hospital room next to Jeffery. He would be in the hospital for over two weeks until his vitals were strong enough for his family to take him home.

He was in a Coma for more than five months; when his baby sister noticed something about him. It looked as though he was awaking from his coma.

Tanya: "Mom, mom; come quick! Jeffery's waking up; hurry up and come!"

17

Jeffery's mother ran up the stairs and into the room. Standing over his bed, she looked into his open eyes and smiled. Though they were blank with no emotion – it was still a gift to her – her son was back from wherever he was. She ordered her daughter to call the doctor and have him come to exam Jeffery.

When the doctor arrived an hour later, he did notice some activities of brain functioning but very little. He would ask that certain items like radio, TV and music be placed next to him. That this was likely to help in the registering and growth of more brain activities as time went by. But, that he was still in a state of coma but not one of sleeping. And, that they try and give him soup with a spoon; and if he was able then it was alright to have the nurse remove the intravenous feeding bags.

When Tanya brought in the radio, he didn't seem to like listening to his favorite station, WBAI 99.5fm where they talked about public concerns of the day. So, she put the record player near him and he again seemed less interested, so, she placed a ten inch TV and cassette player combined and put in a Kung Fu movie for him to watch.

Tanya noticed instantly how his eyes brighten up as though to say 'thanks'. He had only two movies with this theme – 'Five fingers of Death' and the 'Drunken Master' – she would play one movie per day for the first week, until she was able to get down to Chinatown for more movies. When Jeffery received his beating, his Real Estate agent had almost finished the move to Connecticut when he heard about his tragic accident. He'd offer to take that money and put it into a home nearby. He got the family into a two story home in the Village of Tuckahoe. Nearby was the Bronxville Hospital where Jeffery would be taken if an emergency ever arose.

As the years went by, so did grow the collection of his Kung Fu videos. His sister Tanya was now going to the college just up the street; Concordia University where she majored in Medicine. She would make sure her brother got well no matter how long it took. Many more years would go by, and still Jeffery lay in bed with only his eyes opened to see the world go by. But; whenever Jeffery closed his eyes, he could see himself standing in the bedroom practicing his Kung Fu. It was like seeing; but from a different dimension then that before him with his eyes opened.   He was now watching his movies on a big screen TV placed on the wall before him. Doctor Tanya had purchased it for him, as she was now working in the Bronxville Hospital and married to a Pakistani Doctor, Hassan Muhammad.

Dr. Hassan: "Tanya my dear; I cannot understand how your brother, who has been bed ridden for over fifteen year, but his muscle structural is strong! There are no bed sores – which is likely due to the nurses care of him – and his eating mostly liquid vegetables and fruit juices have given him a very good chance of one day walking again. When was his last brain scan done on him Tanya?"

Waleed Yaser

Dr. Tanya: "He had a CAT scan about six months ago and they seemed normal; but we couldn't understand why he hasn't awakened and stood up at least. My mom is positive that one day he will. As for his muscle structure – I guess it due to the many Kung Fu movies he's watched over these many years. I would notice his fingers and toes flinching when the fighting in the movies intensified. It was like he was fighting himself against the foes on the screen. Listen, we are all very positive that one day he'll sit up in bed and ask for some White House Burgers, which were his favorite. Okay honey; we have to go now – mom will bring him his juice dinner and put the movies on so he can watch them all night until he falls asleep." Both the doctors were working the same shift at the hospital. Hassan in the OR and Tanya in Emergency.

It was coming up on 10 p.m. when Jeffery's mother entered the room with his dinner. She had blended chop meat, carrot, celery, potato, red onion, parsley and other vegetables in the Vita-mix blender for his soup. He would drink from the straw all his soup, and when his mother was walking out the door to go back to the kitchen for his fruit juice, something happens to cause her to drop the container.

Jeffery: "Mom; can you put movie in new for me mom."

The first words from his mouth were likening to his very first words as a baby. He spoke the word Momma – she turned as tears began to gush from her eyes – to see him trying to raise himself up to view the TV better.

Mom: "My son lives! Welcome back Jeffery! Momma has missed you for so long, but now my handsome son has returned! Here, let me fix your pillows so you can watch your movies. Is there anything else you want me to give you dear?"

Jeffery: "Yes mom; call Tanya and tell her to come!"

Mom: "I will Jeffery, I will! She'll be surprised – but, I won't tell her why she needs to come – I will tell her I'm concerned about your health, but will let her know there is no danger so she doesn't drive here like some crazy woman. Do you know your sister is a Doctor Jeffery?"

Jeffery: "She is momma; that's good for her. I think saw her standing before me every now and then – the time thing has me confused. How long have I been in bed like this?"

Mom: "Over sixteen years now Jeffery. Your money brought this house for us when you were attacked by those thugs. Do you remember anything about who might've done that to you Jeffery?"

Jeffery: "No mom I don't – just call my sister; I miss her!"

Mom: "Alright I will son. I'll be back in a few minutes with your juice okay!"

Jeffery: 'Yeah, I know who did this to me – his name is etched in my mind and his face in my eyes. He'll get his for sure no matter what! Oh! And what about what's her name, and the baby. I can't remember her name – I wonder what happen to them. When mom returns, I'll ask her if she knows.'

Sitting up in the bed for the first time in years; Jeffery tried to move his fingers and toes, but found it difficult. He would close his eyes and see himself striking a blow into the air with his hands and kicking towards the heaven with a force enough to break a tree branch. Hearing footsteps, he opened his eyes to see his not so little sister standing before him crying with her hand over her mouth. She walked slowly over to him and sat on the bed and hugged him for what seemed a day long.

Dr. Tanya: "Are you here for good Jeffery – you won't go back to sleep on me, will you – anyway I'm glad you're back."

Dr. Hassan: "Hello Jeffery; I am your brother in-law Hassan. I am very happy to now meet you." Shaking his hand Jeffery's grip was weak but firm. "Nice grip you have there, Jeffery. Here, let me look in your eyes. Yes, good response with pupil dilation and motor skills are not bad. Well Jeffery; I think with some physical therapy you can be up and walking in a few months. It will be nice to have you over for dinner. Now, I have to get back to the hospital – I'm on duty tonight with your sister – who also needs to return; we will come by later when we get off work Jeffery. Once again; we are all very happy to see you up and about."

Dr. Tanya: "Okay big brother, we'll see you later. When I get back I'll bring something special for you if you can eat them."

Jeffery: "Sis come here I want to say something in your ear." Tanya came over and leaned so he could reach her ear. "I have a child out there somewhere and I need to know where they are." She rose up and looked him in the eyes and walked out of the room.

Weeks had gone by, and Jeffery was doing well with the physical therapy as he was now walking with little assistance with crutches. He was still unable to walk in a Walker by himself, but was able to stand and support himself. The doctors expected it would take another six months before he could go on his own.

Jeffery never cared to mention to Tanya, about the baby lost in the world and whether there was a way to find out if it was ever born. He would sit in the room, watching TV and thinking back about the old hangout. What had come of his friend Die B and the others? Had they elevated into newer phase of crime or in jail do time. But, what really stuck to him was Jenna. What would she look like after all these years?

His memory of her was vague. He only could picture her in that great body with medium length partial blonde and black hair. Did she know of his near death experience, and did she abort their baby. Why didn't she come to see how he was all these years? He promised himself to get better and go find his family. But, first he wanted to get those who put him here in the first place. It would all start tonight. He would plan and implement his plan with great precision and force! He listened for the moving about of his mother downstairs – and believing she'd not come up, he closed his eyes and stood up tall. He walked over to his closet and opened it. Looking inside for a black pair of pants, a black shirt, a black jacket and a black knitted cap, which he pull down over his face. Hearing his mother now coming up the stairs, he turned and walked briskly back to the bed. Opening his eyes; he fell butt first onto the bed and laid down.

Mom: "Jeffery; I'm making pancakes, do you want to try and eat some solid food?"

Jeffery: "I don't know momma; are they healthy for me – or we could just stick to what got me here in the first place, juices and stuff like that."

Mom: "Yes son; these are very healthy. They are made with buckwheat and flak seed flours, egg whites and butter milk. You'll love them; and I have Vermont Maple Syrup with very little butter for taste. I'll have them ready for you in about twenty minutes. Okay, just sit here and watch your movies. I'll put in your favorite – 'Five fingers of Death'.

When his mother left to continue making pancakes; he closed his eyes and stood up and walked over and took what he needed from the closet. Everything was black down to his socks. Tonight he would go back to the neighborhood and seek out the Italian boys who done what they done to him. His plans were to get one by one until all were either dead or crippled for life.

Standing in the middle of the room; he got into the 'Tiger Claw' stance and practiced for ten to fifteen minutes, or until he hears his mother coming upstairs with the pancakes. His motions were fluent and each strike with his fist was deadly and snapped with a sound of a whip. Standing with one leg reaching for the ceiling, set in motion what would be the kill stomp. Little noise did he make, but with extreme force behind it. Moving about the floor with a graceful like dance, he perfected his kill blows.

His mother would be asleep somewhere around 11 p.m. just after the news, and that would be his chance to go out the window and down the tree. But, how would he pay for the train ride down to the Fordham Road stop. He had no money to say – all was in his mothers care, and how could he ask for something he really didn't need in his condition. He would have to steal from her while she was sleeping, or, maybe ask his sister, but she too will want to know what he wanted with money if he was not able to walk on his own. He had enough hours before that time came up to figure something out.

Jeffery: 'Where can I get the money to travel into the Bronx? I won't steal from mom; anything worth pawning in the house, has to go to the pawn shop, and I can't do that at night. What then, where is the cash coming from? Wait, wait one minute.

My change bottle; it has to be here in the house. I didn't see it in the closet. Maybe it's hidden in some of the other rooms – but, how will I go about looking for it, when mom can come upstairs anytime. I'll have to keep her occupied downstairs for at least an half an hour. I have to give her something to do, that'll keep her hands involved for all that time. What, what can she do to keep her busy – I know, she can make me some of her famous buttermilk biscuits – that's self involved with her hands in all that flour and stuff. "Mom! Can you come up here for a minute please?"

He could hear her footsteps ascending the steps and down the hallway. She stood at the door with a kitchen towel thrown over her shoulder.

Mom: "Yes Jeffery; what do you want?"

Jeffery: "I hope I'm not bothering you momma."

Mom: "No son you're not. I was just in the kitchen putting away the dishes from the dishwasher. What is it that you want son?"

Jeffery: "Well, you know since being asleep for all that time, I thought about something that I really missed – and that is, your hot biscuits smeared soft butter and honey – I can smell them right now. So, if it's not too much of a burden on you momma; could you make a batch for me and just bring them up here along with a pitcher of milk?"

Mom: "Oh Jeffery; I would be very happy to make those biscuits for you. I'll just go back downstairs and start on them now. You'll have them before you before the hour coming. Your momma been racking her brain thinking what she could do for you, and this is an easy task." Turning and walking back down the stairs and into the kitchen, she began working on those biscuits.

Jeffery closed his eyes and stood up and walked out the bedroom. He looked down towards his mom's bedroom and in the other direction of where his sister's room once was. What better place than his sister's room to store items not used every day? Walking down the hallway and into her room, he could see an unmade bed, a dresser and two nightstands. Walking over to the closet, he looked in and around but found nothing. Leaving that room, he walked to his mother's room. Inside he saw it dimly lit with every fixture a bedroom could have. In the closet he found it somewhat cluttered. If the bottle was hidden anywhere, it would be here. Looking about the piles of stuff, he found the bottle nestled towards the back. Inside he found it like he left it – more than half full with quarters, dimes and nickels. Picking it up as not to make too much noise, he turned it over and out spilled about ten dollars. Placing the bottle back and leaving the room, he went back into his room, hiding the change under his mattress, he got back into bed and opened his eyes.

Waleed Yaser

NIGHT STALKER

It was well passed 11 p.m. when he heard his mother go into her bedroom and closed the door. She had checked in on Jeffery and saw him sleeping, so she turned off TV and all the lights in the house. She was a heavy sleeper, so waking up during the middle of the night was not her normal routine.

Getting out of his bed and dressing in all black, Jeffery took the change and put it into his pocket, opened the window and climbed out onto the roof. Throwing his walking cane to the ground, he jumped onto the tree and climbed down. He took notice of the address on the house, and street name at the end of the block. He began making his way to the main street – not being familiar with his surroundings – he walked in the direction he thought would take him to the train station. As he continued to walk, he came upon an older man walking in the opposite direction. Acting as though being blind, he questioned whether he was heading in the direction for the train station. Confirming that he was walking in the right direction, he hastens his pace until the station was within sight. Standing on the platform he saw just a few people waiting along with him. It was coming up on mid-night when the train came into the station. Stepping onto the train, he sat down and waited for the conductor so to pay for the ride.

Aldo: "Pick up for table four; come on girls, let's get the food to the people, and that table also get two pitchers of beer."

Aldo was one of the boys that took part in the punishment on Jeffery. He was now a line cook for the Napoli Boyz Sport and Grill Bar. Paolo who was also there that night controlled the drinks behind the bar. While other members of the gang held different position, Salvatore and Vito were in the office on the second floor of the Sports Bar.

In the basement were items that stolen and then resold. They had become one of the largest hijacking organizations in the area, and used the Sport Bar as a front for what they were really into.

The bar had about thirty tables, along with a forty foot long bar. Every night of the week, but especially the weekends; the place was full and not a table could be found. The place was making from ten grand fifteen grand per night. Along with the stolen items, they were pulling in thirty grand per night. Vito was kicking back ten grand to the bosses so as not to be hassled. All was going great for the Napoli Boyz these past fifteen years. That was, until the visitor came back to town.

In the years gone by; Arthur Avenue had taken on some new changes. It was more a cosmopolitan type area now. Many Latino families had moved in on the north end – thus leaving it accessible for all whom wished to visit – and the entire race problem were now limited to just the hardcore oldies who couldn't give it up. Going in to eat at Napoli Boyz were usually segregated – they'd allowed you to come in and purchase a takeout pizza, but to sit for lunch or dinner – if your skin color was a hue darker then the pizza crust; you'd be looked at all the while you were in eating. Too many of the old-timers wanted to keep things as they once were, back in the early 1960's. And one wonders why this so-called great nation hasn't gotten beyond this sickness.

Old Lady on Stoop: "Hey you! Yeah you; I'm talking to you? What; are you deft and blind – yeah, come over here – walk to your right! Are you lost; did you turn down the wrong street? What are you looking – oh, right; what are you trying to find?"

Jeffery: "I am not sure if I'm lost Ms.. Someone back at Fordham Road said I could get to Southern Boulevard walking this way; is that right and if so, which way should I continue to walk?"

Old Lady on Stoop: "You didn't have to come down Arthur Avenue off of Fordham Road; you could've just kept down Fordham until you got to Southern Boulevard and turned right. What are you; Puerto Rica or Black? Not that it means anything, but I just can't figure you out."
Jeffery: "I'm Latino lady! Listen, I hear tell that it was tough back in the day on this street. I'm not from here; I'm from California. I just moved here a few weeks ago, and I'm trying to familiarize myself with the area. I've been blind for the past ten years now. I won't have any trouble on this street will I?

Old Lady on Stoop: "No, as long as you keep to yourself; and stay out of the way of the Napoli Boyz. They're one bad bunch of boys still – been that way since I was young – always getting into trouble, and now they have that Bar. It's all a front anyway; I know their doing things from the backdoor – especially that Vito! He's the worst of the bunch. He's made you know – that is, he can't be touched unless the Big Bosses give the okay. They even named their bar after them. It's down the street a bit on the left side. Okay, hope you make it home safe and next time keep on Fordham until you get to your street. Goodnight!" She got up and walked into the building.

Jeffery: 'So, they run a bar and are still up to their shenanigans still. I think I'll hang out in the alleyway and see who comes out. Getting them one at a time is how I should handle this. I'll leave Vito for last – he'll suffer the most.'

The time was nearing 2 a.m. when Aldo stepped outside in the alley for a quick smoke. The dinner was slowing down, as most of the patrons were just drinking beers and watching reruns of Italy's soccer games. The bar was half full still, as closing time was 4 a.m. on the weekdays, and 6 a.m. on weekends. Aldo lit up a split and had taken three tokes, when he heard something behind him. Turning to see what it was, out stepped a blind man dressed in black.

Aldo: "Oh, you kind of startled me for a second there. You aren't back there taking a shit are you – because, if you are I'm going to make you clean it up with your shirt – you blind ass fool; now get out of here!" Taking a step towards the back door, Aldo is pulled by the back of his pants by the cane the blind man was walking with. "What; are you crazy or something. I'm going to hand you your ass in a second if you don't let me go!" With one jerk, he was flat on his ass looking up at the blind man.

Jeffery: "You don't remember me do you? I guess not, because you and your friends left me for dead some fifteen years ago – back at that junk yard!"

It all came back to Aldo like a flash of lighting striking the ground. His eyes widen as he forced himself to his feet. He was just as quickly put back down on his ass with a strike to the forehead with an open hand. One second later; a heel kick to the groan area sent a sharp pain to his head that all he could do was to gasp. That was followed downward blow to his heart – stopping it thus causing his death. He then reached into his pockets, and removed his wallet, placing it into his pocket.

Slowly walking out of the alley and heading back towards Fordham Road, he hailed a gypsy cab and asked to be driven back to Tuckahoe, where he would climb up the tree, get inside and undress.

Sometime after Jeffery's leaving of the area; Aldo's body was found in the alley, from what looked to be an accidental fall on his head. They would surmise he tripped while trying to light his split, which lay beside him half smoked. When the police arrived; they looked over the incident and wrote it off as accidental. They had seen no sign of a struggle or any defensive marks on his body as though fending off an attack; so, they closed the case and waited for the meat wagon.

Standing before his bed with the wallet in his hand, he opened his eyes and flopped down onto the bed, where he laid back and counted the cash. He'd really scored big on this one. The guy had more than fifteen hundred dollars In his wallet. He would use this to get around town, while taking out the Napoli Boyz one by one.

Reaching over on the night table, he took the remote control and turned on the TV and DVD player and began watching a movie. This movie had become his favorite since Five Fingers. It was the Jett Li 'Fearless' movie, which had so much violence – he would lay back, close his eyes, and listening with the volume turned up - he would picture himself in every scene, fighting against all foes; and even the most violence of scenes, where he fights with the sword in the restaurant. This movie would cause him to break out in sweat; where his mother would think he gotten a fever because of the wet clothes. He was only perfecting his skills as he walked throughout these movies. He had become a master of the art of Kung Fu!

33

Mom: "Jeffery, wake up boy; you're dreaming again! What do you want for breakfast?"

Opening his eyes; though he was not sleeping but, in a fears battle with one of his foes to the deadly end, he opens his eyes bring him back into reality of the moment.

Jeffery: "Anything you want to cook momma, it doesn't matter to me. Oh, can I have a glass of your vegetable juice also."

That night after his mother went to bed, Jeffery dressed and climbed out the window and made his way to the train station. Back now on Fordham Road, he took a cab to Arthur Avenue and stood outside of Napoli Boyz restaurant watching from across the street. It was Friday night and the street was full of patrons looking to get into the best restaurants for an evening with family and friends.

Jeffery watched as people came and went throughout the night. He had no idea of time, just patience's and a strong will, for one more of the crew was to die tonight. It was during what looked to be an argument spilling out onto the sidewalk that he noticed one of the men arguing was one of the gang members who assaulted him. Seconds later out stepped Vito himself. He took his friend by the collar said something in his ear and went back into the restaurant. The argument stopped as his friend walked off down the street. The other person went back into the restaurant.

Walking down the street on the other side, Jeffery followed him until he came to a Pastry Shop. Going inside and sitting down at the counter; he was served a plate and a cup of what might've been coffee. He sat there for almost half an hour, talking with the young lady serving him. Getting up he reached into his pocket and put a bill on the counter. Walking out again, he looked up towards the Napoli restaurant and continued down the street. Closely behind him walked Jeffery, as people walking in the opposite direction, made way for him, thinking he was blind. He followed the man to an apartment building where he opened the front door with his key, closing it behind him. Standing on the street looking up at the four story building, he waited to see which window the light would go on in. Taking a few steps backwards to get a better view of the side of the building, if his apartment was in the back of the building, Jeffery stood, until he noticed a light go on. It was likely that his apartment was in the back of the building. He would walk around the block to see if he could come up in the backyard and up a fire escape. On the other block was another building like his, which did not give him access without going through the front door. Walking up the steps he looked at the doorbells and rang half of them. Standing there waiting to see if he'd be buzzed in; a young Italian boy came to the door.

Boy: "Can I help you mister? Who are you looking for?"

Jeffery: "Yes you can sonny; is this 987 Arthur Avenue?"

Boy: "No it's not! Arthur Avenue is around the corner to your left. Hey why don't you have a Seeing Eye dog to help you

35

around? Go around the block to Arthur Avenue okay! Good night!"

Letting the door go and turning around to go back into his first floor apartment. Jeffery stuck his cane into the door to keep it from locking again. Walking inside and heading for the basement, which would take him to the backyard of the building, he came up to the back of the apartment where his next victim lived. Locating the apartment, he climbed up the fire escape and into the kitchen window, which was dark. Most likely his victim was either in his room or the parlor. Closing the window behind him – he quietly walked towards the front of the apartment. Down the hallway he stepped listening for a voice he came upon the bedroom which was closed. Not hearing anything, he continued towards the front. He was nearing the parlor, when he heard a voice talking as though he was on the phone.

Dino: "Yeah, I gave him a piece of my mind alright, and then Vito had to come put his two cents in also. This problem is between him and I and not Vito. I can handle my workers with his involvement – he doesn't mess with you and the girls does he? Yeah, you're right – someone needs to step up to Vito – he's been heading this gang far too long – if he wasn't a 'Made Man' I'd clip his ass myself and take over the crew. No don't worry, this is between you and I – it won't get out if you don't say anything. Anyway; I'm going to take a shower and get some sleep. I have to go to Philly tomorrow early and pick up that package. Yeah; we're dealing in counterfeit money now!

We're planning on passing it off here in Manhattan. You have about twenty girls there with you, that will purchase high price items and then we'll sell them out of the restaurant's attic. Anyway; I'll talk with you later okay! Bye!"

Hanging up the phone and jumping up from his seat, he walked down the hallway into the bathroom, leaving the door ajar. Turning on the water he got in and began showering. He was humming something under his breath when Jeffery walked in.

Standing on the other side of the shower curtain he pulled it back exposing Dino's naked body.

Dino: "What the Fuck!" Were the only words he got out his mouth, before Jeffery pushed him, causing him to fall backwards, hitting his head against the tub splitting open his skull. Blood gushed about the tub as Jeffery blocks most of it with the curtain. With the blood on the inside of the curtain, it could only mean he slipped on a bar of soap. But, he wasn't using a soap bar to bathe himself. He was using liquid soap instead – so, Jeffery squeezed half the bottle on his body and into the tub, before dropping it inside. Number two!

Leaving from the same window he came in and walking through the basement he came out of the other building and headed north towards Fordham Road. Again he would hail a cab to take him to Tuckahoe and drop him at the train station, where he would walk home and up the tree into his room. He would sleep till morning when his mother would repeat the same routine. He now had two and with six more remaining before he was finished with this Napoli gang forever.

Later that morning, when Dino didn't show up to drive with Franco; Vito and Salvatore went to his apartment. When they didn't get a response from inside, they broke down the door and entered. Finding the water still running in the tub and Dino's head cracked open, they called the police.

When the police got there they questioned both Vito and Salvatore as to why they thought it necessary to break down the door instead of calling the supper to open it. Their answers left them with much suspicion hanging over them both. The Medical Examiner would rule it an accident and another case would be closed.

Vito and Salvatore would question how two accidents by two gang members would come so close behind themselves. Was the gang's luck running out or was there something sinister behind these occurrences. Franco and Luca would make the trip to Philly to pick up and return back safely. Maybe their luck was still intact and just Aldo and Dino's weren't. They would morn and hold a special night at the bar for them, but still business would go on as normal.

Mom: "Jeffery your sister is coming over today. Plus, your nurse is returning back from vacation, she'll be coming with your sister."

Jeffery: "My nurse from physical therapy is coming here?"

Mom: "No, I'm talking about your nurse who has been taking care of you these past five years now. She comes two to three times a week – more if I'm going out for grocery shopping – she doesn't know of your new condition. She'll be surprised to see you sitting up on your own. She's taken good care of you, so we've kept her these pass years going. You'll like her when you see her. She's Italian but she looks Puerto Rican if you ask me – she might have some of our blood in her.

Jeffery: "Okay momma!" 'I bet she looks like a hag – momma always see's pretty no matter what.'

It was mid-afternoon when Tanya arrived. Jeffery could hear her and the nurse greeting momma when they came in. Walking up the steps he could hear Tanya asking the nurse not to be surprised by what she saw. Thinking nothing in particular, the nurse voice seemed nervously shaken as what she might see.

When the two of them stood in front of the doorway; Jeffery was shocked by the beauty of the nurse. Who upon seeing Jeffery sitting up in bed, awoke and smiling; she fainted right there on the floor. Momma had to come up and help Tanya pick her up and place her in the chair next to Jeffery's bed.

When Tanya gave her smelling salt to revive her; the nurse looked at Jeffery and cried for awhile. Calming down and

39

composing herself, she asked how he was doing and how it felt to be back with his family.

Nurse: "You look great Jeffery – for someone who's been in your condition for as long as you have, you really look good. Do you have any plans for your future mapped out yet?"

Jeffery: "No, that's a bit too early for me to make such decisions until I regain my complete health. I was once thinking about having an auto repair business before this incidence happen to me. I guess I might look into doing that, but for now, I have other things to think about. My mother tells me that you've taken care of me for some time now."

Nurse: "Yes, going on six years now. With your mother's help we made sure you were well groomed and bathe two times a week – no, I know what you're thinking – your mother did most of the special areas; hee hee! But again Jeffery; I'm very happy you are back!" Holding out her hand – he took it and caressed it softly in both hands – looking into her eyes as he did this, something sparked from within and he let go quickly. "Something wrong Jeffery?"

Jeffery: "No, nothing wrong; but, I thought I felt something like an electric shock – small, but electric! Tell me; was your hair always short like that?" She was about to answer, when his sister came into the room with a tray of White House Burgers. There must've been about twenty or more piled up on that tray.

Tanya: "Stop getting fresh with the nurse Jeffery; do you want her to leave just after getting back from vacation. By the way Jenna where did you go? You stay in state or what?"

Jeffery: "Oh, forgive me for not asking your name. Jenna is it; nice to meet you!"

Jenna: "That's okay Jeffery; that could be expected. No, I took my son and we went to Florida to stay with friends from nursing school. I was there for one month and then we went to the Bahamas for a week. I left Jason with my friend's mother – he's going on fifteen now – so, he can take care of himself, which is why I don't worry about him. He's a very handsome boy Jeffery; maybe one day I'll bring him back to meet you, now that you're better."

Jeffery: "Sure Jenna; I'll be happy to meet him! Okay, those burgers are getting cold from all this talk. Let's eat!"

They all stayed in and out of the room for the remaining of the day. When it was getting close to Tanya's work hours, she offered to drive Jenna home before going to work. Accepting the ride, Jenna bid Jeffery goodnight and left. Momma came in and smiled at her son. That smile she'd smile when she knew her son was hot on someone.

Mom: "Don't go getting all hot for her Jeffery; she is your nurse remember. We don't want her losing her job because you can't keep your hands off of her. Anyway; if you want something for dinner tell me now – I'm tired and want to hit the sack sooner than normal. Plus, there's a good movie coming on HBO tonight."

Jeffery: "No momma I'm good; I eat most of them burgers you know. It'll hold me off till morning, but if you like to, could you make me a carrot, apple and ginger drink? They're the best momma!" He couldn't get over how much the two of them connected being it was their first time meeting. There was something about this nurse that made him feel more alive. But; putting those feeling aside – his mind was set for tonight and which Napoli Boy would go down next.

Propped up in the bed, Jeffery waited in the dark, for his mother to go to sleep. But sleep wasn't on her agenda for this night. Whatever movie it was, led into watching another movie and then another. It wasn't until almost 3 a.m. that the TV went off and all was quiet. There was no way for him to go now – he would just double up if he could the following night. Closing his eyes, he stood up and walked down the steps as quietly as he could, trying not to wake his mother, who would be shocked at the least, to see him walking without his crutches.

Down in the kitchen, he looked into the refrigerator for some left over juice and maybe a slice of pie – hunger was setting in and not being able to sleep didn't help. Not only were the thoughts of the Napoli Boyz causing a lack of sleep; but so did his meeting with Jenna, the lovely nurse who'd he figured wasn't really telling the truth about not viewing his 'peace maker' – and most likely when it stood at attention all those years. He might've been inactive; but he wasn't dead either. As he stood with the refrigerator open, his imagination ran amuck. He saw himself in bed, and the nurse coming with a pail filled with water and a rag, where she striped him down to nothing, and began bathing him from foot to the top of his head. He saw himself laying there; eyes open not able to move as his private began rising to where he could view it – she continued bathing his body, as the bed became wet from all the water, he looked again at himself as he was now at full mask throbbing filled with ecstasy awaiting her next move.

She seeing his excitement growing began to undress knowing he was unable to move or to even yell out; she stroked his nature between both hands as his eyes widen either from fear or pleasure, she didn't seem to care either way. She removed her bra and caressed his tool between both breast slowly at first – as he own breathing quicken she could feel the moisture growing between her legs – removing her panty's as they fell upon the floor, she mounted him like a first timer on a pony, careful and assured not to fall, as she made love to him.

With a single tear falling down his cheek from what feelings he might've felt long before his ordeal, spilling from below her mixed with the soapy water under him oozed forth her needs of love. He looked upon her as her eyes closed and her head tilted upwards to the ceiling, looking for who knows what; but still he withheld what was building internally and wanting to release within her a long awaited confession of what they should've had together. His arms, though unable to move, reaching forward just to touch the flesh on her body restrained by a barrier not to cross, soft, warm, as he shakes below and softens to her moves, relaxed spell bent, she dismounts covers her nature and bathes a body laying still sleeping wishing to awaken all sharing never forgetting life's future.

AH! CHOO!

Jeffery: 'Momma's sneezing will awaken her – I've got to get back to the room – in bed and, continue to deceive them until all are dead and forgotten.' Up the stairs he ran quietly pass her door, into his room and in bed, as his eyes opened he laid down thinking it was a wishful vision or a reality brought forward.

Detective Russo: "Listen Vito; we all know you and the Napoli Boyz run things on this block, but whenever there is a murder I step in and run things. You don't want me here in your backyard looking over your fence. You'll never make money and the big Bosses won't receive their cuts – which makes life for you difficult to say the least. I need to know more about what happen to Aldo and if we were to look deeper, we might discover something more with Dino's death also. So, tell me why Aldo had his 'nuts' kicked in? Who would do something like that – uh; you didn't have a beef with him did you?

Vito: "This is the first time I'm hearing that Aldo's nuts were cracked! I know nothing about that Russo! As for Dino; he slipped in his bathtub on body shampoo. What are you fishing for here Russo? If you had something on me concerning this you'd have arrested me already, and I'd be in the interrogation room. But, you have nothing so; I say you just leave and get more evidence before coming to me with this shit! See him out boys! Have a nice day detective!"

Salvatore: "He's trying to pin Aldo's death on us, why then did the rule it an accident in the first place. Now they say he was kicked in the nuts – I don't ever remembering hearing that someone died from a kick to his nuts.

Vito: "Listen up Sal; tell the boys to be more conscious of their surroundings from here on out! Plus, give a call to the G'dfather and ask him if there's a contract on my gang – he'll tell us if there were; but ask him all the same – I don't want any more of my boys taking dirt naps. Now, as far as our business goes; we stay on track with what we have going on this week. Okay; let's get moving now. The bar opens in a few hours – and is everything ready in the kitchen – if not then get them Mexican's moving. I want a flawless dinner service tonight. No mix up's and we stay on point watching each other's ass!"

Concern with the finding of Detective Russo; Vito opened his desk drawer and loaded the 380 semi-automatic. Placing it under the desk, in the shelf for easy access, he leaned back thinking. Who'd want to come after them? All treaties were signed in front of the G'dfather himself. Every gang had their section of Arthur Avenue and they kept to the treaty. They all made money and everyone was happy. The cops were most likely trying to stir things up on the streets again. They wanted the in-fighting between the gangs – they'd rid Arthur Avenue of us they had to political power to do so, everybody got a piece of Arthur Avenue but the cops.

If anyone else from the Napoli Boyz were found dead within the coming weeks; there would be a sit down with the gangs to find out who was sectioning these hits, and that there be payback for not getting authorization from the Boss! It was near sunset, when Vito made a call. He was calling his lawyer to make ready if the cops came back with a warrant for his arrest. Better to plan way ahead then at the moment!

Mom: "Jeffery, Jeffery! I just got a call from an old friend from high school. He's back in town for a week, and he wants to take me out for dinner and a show on Broadway. I told him that you were sick and that….."

Jeffery: "No momma no! I'm alright here by myself! I can get to the bathroom if needed. I got the crutches by the bed and you can bring up a tray of food before leaving. No, go out and enjoy yourself – how late do you expect to be – it's not that I'm rushing you back….."

Mom: "It'll be all night sonny boy! I'll be back in the afternoon tomorrow – I called the nurse and she agreed to come in and make breakfast for you. You two seem to have hit it off the other day, so, now I have to start getting ready. Your momma isn't as young as she once was – it takes awhile longer to beautify oneself. I'll make you some sliders with and without cheese – they won't be White House burgers but they will be good!"

Good for me – she's out of the way for the whole night, so, going and coming won't be a problem. I'll leave just after she does, and prolong my stay down there. It'll give time to pick out the next victim to kill, and maybe even afford me two victims in one night.

The mothers date came around 9 p.m. to pick her up. He came in and sat downstairs until she was ready. They left for their date a half hour later. Jeffery got dress and was out the window by 10 p.m. – he didn't leave through the door, because he didn't have a key – making his way to the train station and then hailing a cab which dropped him off in the middle of Arthur Avenue. The street was bustling with all kinds of people. There was some food festival earlier in the day, and things spilled over into the night. Restaurants were full as people waited in lines for tables within. Even the Napoli Boyz restaurant was filled – they had placed tables on the sidewalk to try and maximize their profit for the day.

Waleed Yaser

Walking down the sidewalk trying not to bump into the people, Jeffery felt this evening would be a difficulty in singling out which was a member of the Napoli gang or just a regular citizen enjoying a night out on the town. Yes, it seemed things had really changed around here. He saw Blacks, Latino's and Asians milling about enjoying the evening festivals.

The Teenager: "Hey mister! Yes you; don't I know you?" A Latino boy around nineteen years old tapped him on the shoulder. Turning and looking over the youngster head. "Didn't you use to belong to that gang, which use to hang out at the park on Webster Avenue? I remember you from there right – I was just five years old then, and my mom use to let us play there and you guys kept the park safe for us kids. Is that you mister?"

Jeffery: "No, no I do not think I'm that person you're referring to. I just moved in this area a few months ago, and I'm trying to learn the city. Being blind forces you to get out and make your own way – because, most times you are alone to figure it out for yourself. But thanks for asking anyway; okay, bye!" Turning to walk away, the youngster took hold of his shoulder again.

The Teenager: "If you like I can help you navigate these crowded streets for you. I'm just out here trying to make a hustle. I escort visitors to this city to the best places to eat. When I bring a group to a restaurant, depending on the number, the owner gives me between ten to twenty dollars per group."

Jeffery: "So, what do you want from me?"

The Teenager: "I need you to do some blocking for me!"

Jeffery: "And what does that entail?"

The Teenager: "Uh!"

Jeffery: "Entail could mean something like; 'what can I do for you' – like what is it that you want me to do sonny!"

The Teenager: "Oh; I get it now! Listen; you stand in a line I place you in and I'll go get the group of people and then place them in line where you're standing. This way the people don't have to get to the back of a line, you understand now! Okay, come with me." Taking Jeffery by the arm and walking him through the crowded sidewalk, he stopped and placed him on a line of people. "Okay now; just stand here and I'll be back in ten minutes with a group of people – we get paid and I'll split the money with you alright. Really mister; you being blind has made my business profitable. Nobody will ask you to get out of line. Okay; I'll be back soon, don't move – well, you can move if the line moves, but don't go from this line okay?" Running down the block throughout the crowd, he disappeared. Standing in line waiting for the boys return, Jeffery noticed up the block a group of men surrounding an older man make their way from one side of the street, to then go into the Napoli Boyz restaurant. Watching as the group entered, leaving outside two men by the door, Jeffery surmised this was likely the big boss of the street. Farther watching as the line moved slowly and his turn to getting into the restaurant neared, Jeffery was pulled by the shoulder again. The teenager had returned, followed by what looked to be ten or more people.

The Teenager: "Okay mister; I got it from here – just go stand over by the telephone pole – oh, your blind I forget, here stand here until I get paid alright."

Standing by the pole, Jeffery continued to look towards the Napoli Boyz spot. The two men continued to stand outside the door watching and waiting. Just then, out stepped the remaining group of men, surrounding the old man as they walked across the street, and headed up a side street disappearing from his view.

Walking down towards the restaurant and standing by the front door – he appeared to be looking inside the window – using his hands as his focus point; he saw Vito standing behind the bar talking and laughing with the customers. He'd pour himself a drink and the people he was talking to.

Jeffery: 'Your ass will soon be mines to destroy Vito. You should've made sure I was dead Vito – now, I've come back to revenge myself. Your last days are nearing for sure…..'

The Teenager: "No, no you can't disappear like that mister. Here's your split – I made fifty dollars on that group and your part is ten dollars – come with me I have another line I need you to stand in. I spotted this group of Japanese business men walking around. They are big spender and love white girl sex. I got the right spot for them. This line here is for the Napoli Boyz restaurant – they not only serve good pizza and beer, but they have live sex in the basement in the back of the alley. Your job is to get in line – it's not that long – and I'll bring back the Japanese to take your place. Salvatore will pay really well for these types of people. Okay; I'll be right back – I have to sell them on eating at Napoli Bar and Tail!" Running back down the street for his meal ticket, Jeffery stood where he was told – which gave him a great vantage point in spotting his next victim. How many faces did he remember from that night in the junk yard. He knew Vito, Salvatore, and working the other end of the bar was Franco; and behind the partition working the pizza stove were both Luca and Paolo – five face to die soon and most likely Santino working the whores in the basement. Picking which to attack first did not present itself to him then. He would have to wait this one out as the night progressed. Grabbing at his shoulder again was the teenager. He had with him five or six – didn't really count them – Japanese well dressed men! The oldest looked to be in his mid-sixties, but with cash in pocket. He handed the teenager what looked to be a couple of hundred dollar bills, before he pushed him out of the line and placed the Japanese there.

The Teenager: "Oh man are we making out like fat rats tonight! Stand here near to the alley – I have to go to the basement door and ask to be let inside. They're really funny about who can go inside from the alley. Special knock for being let in. I'll be right back mister." Watching the teenage knock three times quickly and then two long intermediate knocks was the signal he'd use to enter and take out whoever resides inside.

The teenager was gone for two minutes when he returned with my share of the split. He'd given me five ten dollar bills this time. Though he was getting paid under the table extra for these Japanese, he truly was a 'Hustler'!

Jeffery: "Okay kid, I got to go now. Thanks for the cash – oh, how much did I make – can't see the denomination; so what is it?"

The Teenager: "You have in your hands six ten dollar bills for only twenty minutes of work – now, tell me where you can make that kind of cash in that short of time! You take care mister and get home safe. I spotted a group of either Irish or German – not sure of their nationality but they do have green paper to spend! Bye and thanks again!" Running down the street again hoping to hustle another hundred bucks, the boy disappeared in the crowd.

Jeffery: 'So, three quick knocks and two short ones. Then the door opens and I step in for the quick kill and then leave! You don't have much time between killing him and walking out of the alley without being noticed. I'll give it another twenty minutes for the whores to calm down the patrons and then I'll move in. The man at the door should be lull by the activities going on inside and he'll laps and then gets struck with a death blow to his heart. Another five minutes and then I go!' Knocking at the door as shown by the teenage; Jeffery stood waiting for the door to open. When it did – he knew right away it was Santino.

Santino: "Yeah what do you want blind man; we have no hand outs here – go upstairs and maybe they'll give you a slice of pizza."

Jeffery: "I'm not here for pizza Santino! I'm here for revenge – I'm Jeffery remember me!" With a swift and powerful blow to his chest; Santino dropped to his knees. His heart had stopped that quickly! Closing the door against his face, Jeffery walked back to the front of the alley and turned up towards Fordham Road. Tonight he would only take one life – too many obstacles in the way for another kill. The weekend was up coming and he'd have time to get the others.

Vito: "Another one of my boys killed right under our noses and no one sees anything! He was right downstairs and this happened! How did they get through the door in the first place! Only few people know the knock sequence to get the door open. No one gets to that door unless one of us directs them. So, I want to know who gave out the knock sequence to the killer or killers. The Japanese businessmen stumbled over him as they ran out all to protect their reputations – they didn't come for the pussy only to get caught up in a murder!"

Salvatore: "Listen Vito; none of us would ever give out the secret knock to anyone, unless Santino did it himself – you know, having someone run for him and bring clients – none of them Japanese men came here asking for entrance into the brothel. So, Santino must've been doing some skimming off of the top for his own pockets. And, if that's the case, then he got what he deserved. No one steals from the Napoli Boyz – if we check his apartment we might even find who he was sliding with behind our backs."

Vito: "All that doesn't really matter at this moment Sal; we have the Detectives coming and they'll be up our asses investigating why none of us heard anything. They know no patron can enter without acceptance from us in the restaurant. Every one of us has to have their stories straight with no variance whatsoever! Have the girls been told what to say and what not to say Sal? If not, go make sure they keep to it – we don't need any more mishaps – the rest of you get to straightening up the bar before they come."

Paolo: "Uh, Vito; he's already here and they brought the army with them!"

Detective Russo: "Well, good morning Napoli Boyz! I guessed you never thought you see me back here so quickly. And I guess you boys don't know what happen either. And, I guess you're wondering why I brought so many officers with me today, right! I sure hope you boys did some house cleaning before we got here – because, I have a warrant to search these premises from top to bottom." Laying the warrant on the bar countertop in front of Vito; he motioned for his men to commence the search.

Vito had already remove any incriminating evidence, and watched as the police made mockery of his establishment. They looked into ever crack, tore down what was thought to be a false wall, yes, the Napoli Boyz were violated to the utmost!

Detective Russo: "Vito; you can come downtown with me to answer some questions on your own, or you can expect a warrant with your arrest for the mysterious murder of Santino – yes, I said murder! Accidental deaths at this location are very unlikely. I will be looking for you later this afternoon in my office Vito; you better bring a good lawyer with you." Throwing his card on the bar countertop, he walked out the restaurant and drove off. Passerby's would look into the windows and then walk on their way.

Vito: "Someone get Siseman on the phone for me; I'm going downtown and I want him there before I get there. You guys replace everything and get ready for tonight's business. Paolo you will replace Santino in the brothel and Luca you take care of the bar. You can get one of the Mexican's out of the kitchen to help pour the beer, while you mix the drinks. I don't know how long I'll be downtown, but remember to keep a close eye out for hit men. I still don't know if the G'dfather has sanctioned this or someone is going rouge." Walking out and getting into his Mercedes Coupe, he drove downtown to be interviewed for the deaths in his establishment.

Lying in the bed half woke from listening to the replay of 'Chopped' and 'Diner, Drive Inn's and Dives' on his new favorite channel (The Food Channel) to watch – he heard the doorbell ring and then the key turn the lock. Most likely it was the Nurse Jenna, who'd agreed to come by and make breakfast for him.

Jeffery: "Is that you down there Jenna?"

Jenna: "Yes, it's me Jeffery! Your mother asked if I could make breakfast for you." Coming up the stairs and standing at the door; Jenna was nicely dressed in Jeans and a tight blouse, showing off the round breast and bulging nipples. "Is there anything special you want to eat Jeffery?" Holding her hands on both hips, with a slight tilt of her head, she smiled!

Jeffery: 'Girl; if you only knew! I'd pour honey over your body and lick you from head to toe – no, honeys too sweet – yes, whip cream spread over your entire body with cherries placed on the erogenous zones, I'd lick and eat my way into your heart.' "Uh, I like pancakes with sausages if you know how to make them from scratch – momma doesn't use box mix!"

Jenna: "Yes, I know how to make them Jeffery – I'll make you a glass of juice also – anything in particular you'd like?"

Jeffery: "Yes, carrot, apple and ginger root with a splash of honey!"

Turning to walk back downstairs; Jenna looked back to see if he was watching her ass. Seeing that he was, she went down and made his drink, so she'd have a reason to return so quickly to him. But unbeknownst to him, she had purchased some illegal Viagra pills and mixed one into his juice. She would corner him for sure; and put herself in the right condition to make love to him. His mother was gone for awhile and no one would bother them.

When she brought him the juice she told him to drink up because she wanted to help him into the sit down shower his mother installed for him way back when he first came from the hospital. She guided him as he walked on his crutches into the bathroom. She helped him remove his pajamas, as he sat inside and turned on the water. He would bathe in his underwear's and replace them before getting out of the shower. When she came back to him after thirty minutes or so, he didn't want to get out of the shower while she was there.

Jeffery: "No Jenna; I can get out on my own – just leave my bathrobe and I'll come into the room in a few minutes."

Jenna: "Okay Jeffery if you want! I'll be in the room waiting for you to help you get dressed. I put some clothes out for you – a warm-up suit with a hoodie to keep you warm."

Waleed Yaser

Leaving the bathroom and him now alone, he could not understand why his thing was all of a sudden harder than a light pole. He wasn't thinking about her; or was he while he showered. He sat trying not to think about anything, especially her – as he waited to see if it would deflate so he could get back to his room. He was now sitting for more than fifteen minutes, when she knocked at the door.

Jenna: "Jeffery is you alright in there – I don't hear you moving about – do you want me to come in?"

Jeffery: "Uh, yes I'm alright, just grooming my hair that's all! I'm coming out now alright!" Knowing he couldn't stay there all day waiting for it to go down, he wrapped the towel around him and put on the bath robe and came into the room. Sitting on the opposite side of the bed, he tried to hide the fact from her. He'd be embarrassed to have her see it – but thought why not she's a nurse – so, he hid it from her.

Jenna: "Here, let me help you with your under wares Jeffery. Here, see if you can hold your legs out."

Jeffery: "No, no Jenna don't do that – oh; I'm sorry you have to see that!"

Jenna: "Oh! Jeffery you're so large – is this all for me – are you coming on to me Jeffery?"

Jeffery: "I'm sorry; but I can't get it to go down! I have no control over it! It happen when I was in the shower. I wasn't thinking about you Jenna, I want you to know that!"

Jenna: "Well Jeffery; I was hoping that it is because you were thinking about me! I'm not embarrassed by this Jeffery – here, let me do something to help it go down." She stood up and began taking off her clothes!

Jeffery: "Uh, Jenna! That's not helping anything – you're only making it worse for me…..what the hell girl! Here, come here!" She was naked standing before him, as she moved closer to him. She took the robe and pulled it down – pushing him on his back, she took the robe from under him. Closing his eye, he pushed himself towards the middle of the bed, where she straddled him like a rider on a horse, and inserted his hard joy stick within her. "Yes, baby girl yes! Move like that, slow, slower; yes, like that!" Taking both breast within his hands, caressing then softly as her nipples harden between his fingers. He rubbed her body all over, as she continued to grin down on his joy stick searching for her climax – which was eluding her every move she made. His eyes still closed – a flash back went throughout his brain so quickly that he couldn't identify its content.

Jenna: "Help me Jeffery; help me get it, help me get it Jeffery! Move your ass man, move your ass! It's coming, it's coming…. yes, keep moving like that, don't stop….yes, yes……ahhhh! Okay stop I got mines!"

Jeffery: "What! Stop! I didn't get mines yet – what about me Jenna? Why don't you help me get mines?"

Jenna: "Not to worry Jeffery; you'll be hard like that for some time now! When I come back from cooking and you've had your breakfast we can go at it again. I gave you something to help keep it like that for the next few hours. It'll ware off by noontime – so, until then; let me get some rest and we'll go back at it with vitality boy."

Jeffery: "What did you give me?"

Vito: "What kind of shit are you giving me Detective Russo! For the last time; I had nothing to do with killing either of my friends. We've been together for over 30 years now – ours is one of the oldest clubs still around on Arthur Avenue – and we'll still be there when you retire Detective Russo!"

Detective Russo: "You mean gang right; not club! Listen, you guys have been running all kinds of illegal activities from your restaurant. But when dead bodies start showing up on your doorstep, then, we have to step in and hassle you a bit. If you don't want your business in the papers then, take your dirty work elsewhere and not on Arthur Avenue. If another body shows up in your area, we'll be obligated to shut you down for awhile. And, if that happens who'll pay the G'dfather off? He's already told me he has not sanctioned such matters on the street, and he's wondering whether you can control it or does he have to intervene. If he has to; then you'll be seeing me again! So, let's try and keep the Avenue clean okay – no more dead bodies! Now get out of here and take that shark with you – nothing personal Lawyer Siseman.”

Vito: “If you want Russo; you can put one of your men in the restaurant to watch over things – I have no problem with that if it’ll keep the Boss happy - send him tomorrow night and have him check in with me. Come on Siseman!”

Jeffery: “So, how long did you say this will last Jenna?”

Jenna: “Oh, about an hour or more now. What, did you just eat a breakfast of champions – did it give you the extra energy to sustain another round with me? What should we start with first Jeffery? You want to go back to 69 or just get on top of things?” Taking off her clothes again and walking around to the other side of the bed – she got in and pulled the covers over her.

Jeffery held her close and kissed her passionately. It felt right, natural like it was meant to be. All those years he said to himself – wasted because of a life style and here he could’ve had someone just like her. Would he have changed his life to be with a woman like her? He might’ve if the timing was right.

Jeffery: “You know Jenna; this feels right with me – you being a part of my life that is – tell me; do you feel the same?”

Jenna: "It's always been this special for me Jeffery! I'm just happy that you're back to enjoy it for yourself!"

Jeffery: "What do you mean 'always special for you' – I don't understand your meaning Jenna!"

Jenna: "Listen Jeffery; I'm going to tell you something and you must promise not to freak out on me, alright!" Jeffery nodded affirmatively as he looked suspiciously into her eyes. "Okay; it's like this Jeffery! We were once nearly husband and wife; that was before they attacked you and you almost died. You and I use to have secret dates which lasted for more than two months. When I heard that Vito and his crew had done that to you; I knew he'd be coming for me also. I was on my way out of town – though I wanted to stay and see after you; but I couldn't because I had something to protect. And, before I could leave he caught me and beat me badly. I almost lost our baby from that beating – had he known I was pregnant he would have killed the baby inside me himself. I got to the hospital and they said all was well – so, after that I left Arthur Avenue and moved upstate to Middletown New York. There I studied until the baby came and afterwards went to Nursing School for three years, got my degree and worked in a hospital in the Catskill area, until I had enough experience to come back down here to take care of you. I had monitored your recovery after they first found you. You know it was a dog that heard your moans from behind the fence – they said if you had gone another hour or more bleeding like you were, you would've died. I must say one more thing – I had taken a vow of chastity until I would return to you. So, when I started working here, I'd wait till your mother went out and I'd ride you until I reached climax. No one ever found out about us – and, they will not find out until the time is right. We'll just keep doing what we are now doing until you have fully recovered. We have the right to have our own life Jeffery!"

Jeffery: "What is the child's name Jenna?"

Jenna: "His name is Joseph like the prophet in the bible. He's almost fifteen years old – he's very handsome and kind of tall for his age – maybe he'll be a basketball star; but, I would prefer he study medicine and become a doctor!"

Jeffery: "He can grow to be whatever he wishes Jenna. You know something; I kind of felt we had had sex before – I had this vision about it the other day – it was so surreal! Yes, we'll have our own life Jenna – but first I have to get my revenge for what they did to me – and then we'll take the time out to make a life for us and our boy Joseph!"

Jenna: "And how do you expect to get revenge, when you're still bed ridden – you can barely have sex, and you want to get pay back! How! Just tell me how you're going to do that – pay someone to hit each one of them?"

Jeffery: "Well, Jenna; just like you want me to keep our thing a secret. Well, I also have a secret. One that is somewhat supernatural – one that is unbelievable but true – and it is that

I am not bed ridden; I walk but with special powers. How it happen I do not know, but I am able to walk and fight like a Kung Fu Master! And, I do all this while I keep my eyes closed. Here let me show you!" Sitting up in the bed, closing his eyes he stood up on the floor and did a back flip without hitting the night table or making too much of a sound. He took his left leg and raised it towards the ceiling and held it for over two minutes, all the while talking to Jenna and without losing his balance. It all started when they put on these movies for me to watch while in the state I was in….."

Jenna: "Yes, I remember having to change the movies for you – you laid there with your eyes just fixed on the screen – I didn't know whether you were sleep on in a maze within your mind. So, you must've been exercising in a metapsychology state, thus creating a metamorphous of your body structure, where a person bed ridden like you could maintain their muscle structure all the while. G'd must have been good to you Jeffery – sending that dog and then allowing you to learn this art while in a sleeping mode. Why won't you open your eyes Jeffery?"

Jeffery: "Now; that's the mystery Jenna! When I open my eyes, I lose my balance – but with my eyes closed I not only can walk but, I can see everything before me like in a shadow. I want you to keep this to yourself – a promise that is binding between us."

Jenna: "I promise Jeffery I will!"

Jeffery: "Now; also you must never tell anyone that I have been going down to Arthur Avenue these past few nights, and have already killed three of the Napoli Boyz. I have five more that I will take care of as soon as I have the opportunity. Getting close to them is difficult – but I get close because they don't remember me and they don't fear a blind man – the people think I'm blind because I walk the streets with my eyes closed and plus I have the cane, which I use as a weapon. As soon as the Napoli Boyz are dead, the sooner we can start our new life. This house is yours as it is mines. I will build an addition to the house for mom to live in, and we'll have the main house for ourselves. I should be well enough by year's ending. Okay; enough talk, let's get busy with the sex – momma should be coming soon!"

Under the covers they played trying to recoup the lost and almost forgotten emotions they once shared. With his eyes closed his strength was immense as he took her from one position to another. The bed creaked and moved having not locked the wheels – as they went at making love in a hard poetic kind of way. Every motion of his back, swayed like a Ocean wave, smashing up on the shore and retreating back awaiting the next huge wave. She moaned and groan with passion, and pain as her fingers dug into his back trying to hold on.

Salvatore: "Alright you guys! Come let's get the kitchen and the front of the bar ready for tonight. Make sure all the new table clothes are on each table, and remember to vacuum the curtains and the carpet. Shine all the mirrors and pay close attention to the bathrooms this time. The past couple of days, I've seen it get a bit sticky in that men's bathroom. Those tiny pricks have been coming up short on the urinals with sprinkles on the floor – I'm not having that again this time around. Someone has to check to make sure it is clean on the floors – as for the girl's room; just make sure there are enough of them girly things for them to use. It's 7 a.m. now and I want this place ready to open for lunch and dinner by 11 a.m. Okay, let's get to work!"

Paolo: "Salvatore; do you want me to send the girls downtown now with the counterfeit money?"

Salvatore: "How many girls are going and how much cash does each one have with them?"

Paolo: "I have eight of my most pretties' girls going and each has twenty thousand in cash each. Half of them will shop in the Diamond District and the other will shop on the Upper East Side around Sixtieth Street and Park Avenue. We should make out like a fat rat – especially with the Diamonds and Gold."

Salvatore: "That's good Paolo; just make sure the girls know, that their doing double duty and will be paid handsomely for their work. Also, I want you to know, that the Russians are bringing in another load of girls for us to look over. Our business is predicated with beauty and mostly all our girls are blondes, and our clients love blonds, so, we'll need at least five more to work for us. Just make sure their plump in the rump – don't need any sticks working for us Paolo. If you need anything; Vito and I will be in the office. Now, let's make some money fellows!" Walking from the main lobby, up the stairs to the office, Vito sat behind the desk thinking about what if another murder did happen tonight. Would he hide the body and dump it somewhere far from the restaurant. And, if it was another one of his boys; who could he place the blame upon. Were some people out there looking to maneuver their way into his business? Or is it someone from his past – coming back to seek revenge – but who; he never left his enemies walking so to come back years later. No, this had to be random not planned – but on a whim! He would have eyes roaming about the restaurant for some time to come.

Vito: "This place will be in lock down tonight Sal! All things have to be approved first with one of us, before allowing anyone into the brothel. There will also be no selling of stolen items on these premises until further notice. We will have a few other eyes watching to make sure no one is killed. Okay; let's get ready for tonight pal!"

Jenna: "Jeffery; I just heard from your mother. She says, she will not be coming home until Sunday morning. He's taking her to Atlantic City for a few days, and that I should stay here and watch you. I told her I would but I have to call my babysitter and ask her to keep Joseph for a couple of days. He likes staying with her – her son is the same age, so they have a lot in command – video games and stuff. Plus, that'll give us more leisure time together – we can sit in the media room and watch TV."

Jeffery: "Listen Jenna; I have to get ready for tonight – I need to end this ordeal as soon as I can – I'm hoping to catch them all together and finish them as they tried to finish me. I will be out all night until dawn. The restaurant closes at 6 a.m. on the weekend so; catching them at the last moment in the restaurant is what I hope to do. Hopefully; all this will end tonight – and I'll be able to start my life anew with my family I've just come to know. Jenna; you could cook something for lunch though, and, we'll eat downstairs in the dining room. Afterwards we can sit and watch some movies, until the time that I have to leave is near."

Detective Russo: "Send officer Capri to monitor the restaurant; and tell him to check in with Vito the owner. He knows I'm sending one of my men down to sit incognito amongst the patrons until closing. Tell him it's a Sport Bar and to dress appropriately as not to stick out."

All surveillance tactics were in place for tonight. If anything happened the police would be there to respond immediately with deadly force if necessary. Arthur Avenue would once again be the nice quiet neighborhood it was for so many years. It had gone through much in the past until the G'dfather stepped in and divided things up between the rival gangs. It was now; with these two murders and possibility a third reverting back to the ugly days no one wanted to revisit. Detective Russo would make sure it didn't go back in time – he would nip it in the bud; and if had to, close down the Napoli Boyz forever. There was always a rival waiting in the wings to replace them.

Jenna and Jeffery sat in the media room; chatting about what she had done to get her and his son through the many pitfalls of housing, school and work. He consoled her for not being able to be there for her and his son, and how those who took him for these past fifteen years away from his family, would surely have to pay dearly. His anger would rise, and she would bring him back down with a simple hug and kiss. The pain they both felt was now subsiding with hopes that the near future would bring about a rebirth of life.

Hours passed by without noticing the time. It was coming up on 8 p.m. and the sun had already set. They would sit for another hour – allowing the avenue to get into its weekend mode – crowds of people looking to enjoy life, food and decadent activates for the soul! He would dress with her help

– no longer in black, but with clothes that were torn in places and smudged to make him look homeless. A disguised to get him closes enough to pounce on them in one swoop. His plan was to wait until all the patrons were gone and while they were closing out the receipts for the night, he'd gain entrance and reveal himself and finally rid the world of them. He would bring hell down upon them as they had tried to do for him. The Boyz would be done with at last!

Making his way to the train station and then walking from the Fordham Road station, he turned onto Arthur Avenue. As he walked farther into the street, he could see people milling about the busy street. Coming up on the apartment buildings which were a block away from the business section, he met again that old woman sitting on her stoop. Recognizing him and seeing he was now going through hard times, she kept quiet as he passed on his way down the street. He not wanting to acknowledge her presence continued walking with his cane out in front.

When he got on the corner; he stood looking about for anything out of place – feeling as though eyes were now on him; he located a garbage can to sit on for the time being, or until they chased him away. Holding a plastic cup as if asking for hand outs – he waited as the hours passed and his cup grew heavy. Even from where he sat – he could see that teenager doing his business again – making people happy and getting paid for it. The streets were alive and bustling as the noise level grew by the hours and minutes pass.

Looking into the window of the Napoli Boyz restaurant from across the street; he could see they were very busy and even the alley way had the men coming and going all night long. Not once did he notice the police paying attention to their bar, only walking up and down the street maintaining order of the night. Every now and then he would ask a passerby the time. He had been out there on his perch for more than five hours – it was nearing 4 a.m. and the amount of people dwindled a little but still the regulars maintain a presence on the fairway. As the numbers of men coming out of the brothel lessen; Jeffery thought the time was nearing for him to leave this seating and walk over and find a place in the alley to hide until closing time came. There were too many places back in the alley – one was the large stack of beer cartons waiting for the arrival of the sanitation trucks – which hopefully were well after he'd finished here.

Walking across the street, into the alley, he hid behind the cartons and waited. He would wait for more than two hours, as the men leaving the brothel started slowing down as the minutes passed. When what he thought was the last group of men left the brothel, he came out from behind the cartons and walked over to the door. Knocking on it, he waited for it to open.

Paolo: "What the...no mister we don't serve your kind down here; go up to the front door and they may have leftovers for you. And how did you know the secret knock....unless, you're

71

that guy……" Forcing the bottom of the cane into his mouth to silence him; Jeffery pushed his way in and closed the door behind him. Holding him down with the cane in his mouth and a foot on his chest, Jeffery listened for activates upstairs. Hearing only few footsteps, he surmised that they were now closed and would be waiting for this guy to come up with the receipts for that night. Looking around for where he might've kept the cash, instead he asked him.

Jeffery: "If you want to live to see the next sunset; tell me where you keep the money hidden. Just point to where it is." The guy pointed at the metal box on the table underneath the phone. "Just sit there and hold this in your mouth – if you remove it I'll kill you." Walking over and grabbing the box he opened it and took out the cash. It must've been over twelve thousand dollars in fifties and hundred dollar bills. "How much pussy you guys selling down here – damn good business if you ask me – now, just sit here until your boys come looking for you. I want all of them down here for what is going to be the prelude of a rebirth of my life. You don't remember me do you – I said the same thing to your other three friends, and they didn't know either until I told them. Afterwards, I killed them and likewise will the rest of your crew meet the same fate. I'm Jeffery the gang leader of the Black Dragon's – the guy you and your friends tried killing by hurling broken glass bottles at me in that junk yard. Do you remember me now?" He nodded his head to affirm he did. When he did, Jeffery jammed the cane further into his mouth causing him to pass out.

He stood there removing some of the clothes he worn – as he readied himself to fight those who came to investigate the whereabouts of this guy. It took more than ten minutes or more, before the phone rang. Leaving it ringing he listened for the footsteps above. Hearing them now scurrying about – he knew it was any second that the door would open and they'd come see what was going on.

Voice: "Paolo are you down there – why didn't you answer the phone – Paolo, are you down there! He's not answering me; we have to go down and find out what's wrong. Grab your shit and come!" Footsteps heard descending the steps – walking towards the back of the basement; Jeffery stood in a pair of black tights a one piece suit holding his cane. "Paolo we're here; where are you at?"

Jeffery: "He's over here lying on the floor – which one of you is Vito?"

Vito: Holding the gun in his hand; he pointed it at the blind man standing before him. "What the fuck are you doing blind man – do you know who you're fucking with? You come into my establishment and do this – you'll never walk out of here alive blind man. There are four of us standing before you – oh, that's right you can't see. Are you ready to die now?" Placing a silencer over the barrel of the gun he held it out to shoot. But, before he could pull the trigger, Jeffery knocked out the lone light bulb above his head. Making it an even ground as he went about killing each one of them with lighting fast kicks and blows to the bodies. Gunshot flashes went off two or three times as Jeffery dodged them as they flew pass his head and body.

Striking each of them with powerful blows, one could hear bones brake cries of pain and last gasp of air of life leave some of the bodies. Finally grabbing Vito by his hand and removing the gun by dislocating his arm; he took him to the ground and looked into his face. In the dark Vito saw nothing but smelt fear coming from his body. He'd laid there with the blind man holding him wondering what his next move might be.

Vito: "So, now what! Go ahead and finish me off! I'm not afraid to die!"

Jeffery: "No, you won't die until you know the reason way. You once tried to kill me – back in that junk yard so many years ago – and now I've come for my revenge. I'm Jeffery the Black Dragon leader! But, before I do that; I want you to know, that Jenna lives with our child, and she asked me to say this one thing to you. She wants you to know that, she always thought you were nothing but a racist who hated anyone not Italian. And, that she was happy that she got away from you when she did. Oh, she said one more thing; she hopes you burn in hell!" Choking him with one hand until his struggle ceased; Jeffery got up and walked out of the basement. It was sunrise when he walked out of the alley and headed towards Fordham Road. His pockets were large; from what he took off Vito and the others. He walked off with more than fifty grand easily.

Taking a cab back to Tuckahoe he rang the bell and waited for Jenna to answer. When she saw him she grabbed him and drugged him into the house. The door closed behind them and the past too closed behind them. All that was left was to start a new life as one.

Days later when his mother got home, he told her about Jenna being the mother of his child Joseph, and that she was a Grandmother.

Mom: "What do you two take me for? Jenna when you first came here looking for the job I wanted to give you a chance with the credentials you brought with you. But, when you first brought your son over I knew right then! This is my son and he's been with me since a baby. And when you brought in that nine year boy of yours for the day; I knew right then that this was Jeffery's son. Jeffery at that age looked exactly like your son – with the exception of the green eyes – I wanted you to be close to Jeffery as those people had kept him from you for so long. No, nothing gets pass mother dear. Now, go get my grandson and come home girl!"

Detective Russo: 'I knew these boys were heading for nothing but trouble. Now that they found it – I can clean up this mess and close the case at the same time. I'll file it under mysterious circumstances!'